"This marriage is over."

"Don't worry, Connor," Chelsea choked. "I'm leaving tonight. I'll go back to Grace's."

Connor just shook his head, totally dazed. He gazed into Chelsea's eyes. "How did we get here, Chels? I mean, just a few weeks ago we were happily married. We were poor, but happily married." Connor breathed, cradling his head in his hands, his fingers in his flaming hair. "This marriage is in serious jeopardy," he said.

"No," Chelsea corrected, though the words cut through her like a knife. She rose and started walking home, hugging her arms tightly across her chest. "No, Connor," she whispered shakily. "This marriage is over."

Look for these titles in the **Ocean City** series:

Ocean City
Love Shack
Fireworks
Boardwalk
Ocean City Reunion
Heat Wave
Bonfire
Swept Away
Shipwrecked
Beach Party
*Ocean City Forever**

*coming soon

And don't miss

BOYFRIENDS GIRLFRIENDS

Katherine Applegate's romantic new series!

#1 Zoey Fools Around
#2 Jake Finds Out
#3 Nina Won't Tell
#4 Ben's In Love
#5 Claire Gets Caught
#6 What Zoey Saw
#7 Lucas Gets Hurt
#8 Aisha Goes Wild

BEACH PARTY

Katherine Applegate

HarperPaperbacks
A Division of HarperCollins*Publishers*

This is a work of fiction. The characters, incidents, and dialogues are products of the author's imagination and are not to be construed as real. Any resemblance to actual events or persons, living or dead, is entirely coincidental.

HarperPaperbacks *A Division of* HarperCollins*Publishers*
10 East 53rd Street, New York, N.Y. 10022

First HarperPaperbacks printing: June 1995

Printed in the United States of America

HarperPaperbacks and colophon are trademarks of HarperCollins*Publishers*

❖ 10 9 8 7 6 5 4 3 2 1

A special thanks to Liana Cassel

One

This can't possibly be real, Kate Quinn thought as she watched the enormous sailboat approach their island. She thought that getting stranded in the first place was crazy. But this was even more frightening.

The sailboat was inside the farthest reefs and close enough to drop anchor. On the bow stood a man in a white suit, with a panama hat shading his face from the sun. Kate shivered as she recalled the eerie feeling she and Justin had had when they'd met that man only a week or so ago. Trevor Chernak. The mysterious benefactor who'd paid to have Justin's boat fixed.

Kate felt sick as she remembered the cool drinks Trevor had so politely offered them as they sat by his pool. He didn't look polite now,

Kate knew, her eyes flicking to the men who stood by him, rifles in their arms.

"Justin," she choked. She reached out beside her, and her hand found Justin's, their fingers threading tightly. All of her anger at him disappeared instantly. The only thing left was fear. Funny how a strange boat with a crowd of armed men could do that to a girl.

"Oh my god, Justin, they're coming here, aren't they?" Kate bit her lip and blinked back her tears.

Justin squeezed her hand as he crouched in the sand next to his dog, Mooch, who was trembling and whimpering.

"He knows we're afraid," Justin whispered. "It's okay, boy," he said softly, running his fingers through the shaggy hair. "It's okay."

But it's not! Kate wanted to scream. *I can't believe it's all going to end here.*

It seemed like it was years ago that Kate had decided to fly down to the Bahamas and join Justin. All they were going to do was sail his boat back to Ocean City. It had taken her a long time to make that decision, because she'd been worried about her emotions. About love. About being with Justin again and hoping their future could finally work out. Third time lucky, right?

She'd never really stopped to consider the possible dangers.

So how was it that they now stood waiting for a group of gun-toting drug dealers to take them prisoner? Or worse.

Suddenly Kate heard Allegra sobbing behind her, and it all fell together. Kate whirled around to stare at the pretty suntanned girl standing behind them on the sand.

This was when all the trouble started. The night Allegra Wolfe had "bumped into" their waiter at dinner. *Oh that pathetic story you told*, Kate thought, cursing herself for being so gullible.

When Kate and Justin had first met Allegra, she looked like a sweet, naive teenager, with thick black-rimmed glasses, oversized clothes, and a lopsided ponytail on the top of her head. *It was all an act, though, wasn't it?* Kate thought.

As soon as they'd offered to bring Allegra back to Ocean City with them, Kate's suspicions had begun. It didn't take very long for Allegra to let down her hair, "lose" her glasses, and slip into some decidedly sexy clothes, like the little white bikini she was wearing now; the little white bikini she'd had on when she managed to crash Justin's boat into a reef and strand them on this island.

"I can't believe you, Allegra!" Kate exploded. "You lied to us, and you used us, and now look what you've done. You've put us all in danger. We're going to die on this stupid deserted—"

"Kate, stop it!" Justin grabbed her from behind. "We're not going to die."

"How can you say that!" Kate cried, shaking him off and stumbling away awkwardly on her swollen ankle. "Chernak went to a lot of trouble to hide his drugs in your boat. And he's followed us this whole way because he thinks the drugs are still there. When he finds out that you and Allegra tossed a million dollars' worth of cocaine—his cocaine—into the ocean, what do you think he's going to do? Offer us a ride home and another round of ice tea?"

"He's going to kill us," Allegra whispered, her eyes wide with fear.

"Don't say that!" Justin yelled.

"Why not?" Allegra whimpered. "It's the truth."

Mooch was barking madly and running in circles around them. Justin caught him by the back of the neck and tried to calm him again.

"Why did you have to crash us here!" Kate wailed at Allegra. "Why did you have to trim the sails or change course or do whatever you did! You brought us here and made us sitting ducks. This was your plan, wasn't it? I don't believe you didn't know about the drugs!"

"But I swear I didn't." Allegra stomped her foot vainly into the sand. Her fiery auburn hair flew back from her face, and her small body shook. "Kate, listen—for once, just listen. If I'd known about the drugs, why would I have come on the boat with you in the first place? Why wouldn't I have just flown up to O.C. and taken them there?"

"I don't know," Kate shrieked. "Because this is all part of your plan. All of this." Kate swept her arms around to include the island and the remains of Justin's boat, which they could see bobbing in the water, stuck on the nearest reef. "You meant to crash us here, so that Chernak could get the drugs from us."

"What's he going to do with them in the middle of the ocean?" Allegra cried, her voice cracking with frustration. "Kate, if he stowed them in your boat, *the whole point* was to get them *into the U.S.*! Why would he want me to stop you now? It doesn't make any sense."

"And of course you know all about what makes sense in the drug trade," Kate snapped.

"I don't know anything about the drug trade," Allegra sighed. "But I do know Chernak. He and I have old business, and it has nothing to do with drugs. Don't you get it?"

"Yes, I 'get' your old business, Allegra," Kate said coldly. The image of Justin and Allegra embracing in the moonlight flashed through her mind. "You've been doing the same thing here with us the whole time. I know what you're trying to do with Justin—"

"Stop it! Enough!" Justin cried. "Look, will you?"

They turned to see the big white sailboat dropping its anchor. A swarm of men were preparing to lower two small outboard boats into the water.

"Can we stop arguing for two minutes about whose fault this is,"—Justin glared at Allegra—"and figure out what the hell we're going to do?"

"Do?" Allegra laughed shrilly. "What do you think we *can* do? Maybe if we just start running, they'll follow us. We'll go around and around, and pretty soon they'll get tired and give up, and then we'll hop on their boat and sail away? I think I've seen that one on *The Three Stooges*, Justin. But we're not the Stooges. Like Kate said, we're the Three Sitting Ducks."

"Oh my god," Kate moaned as four men dropped into each of the two small boats. Chernak stood above them, and they could hear him barking orders to his men. "Here they come."

"There's nothing we can do," Allegra said tightly, her eyes darting frantically right and left. She took a step away from Kate and Justin and started muttering. Kate strained to hear her.

"What am I going to say," Allegra was whispering. "I need to think . . . think . . . think . . . what can I say . . ."

"Here we are on the verge of death, and she's still trying to figure out a way to get herself out of it," Kate said. "I don't care what she says. She knew. I'm sure of it."

Suddenly Kate felt strong, warm hands on her shoulders and her eyes filled with tears.

"Stop it, Kate," Justin whispered as he turned her toward him. "Stop thinking about her. Please." His voice was on the verge of cracking. "Just be with me now. Be with me."

Kate buried her face in Justin's shoulder, and the tears came uncontrollably. It was a joke, wasn't it? This wasn't real. It couldn't possibly be real. They couldn't die now. Not now, when it had taken them so long to get back together.

"Oh, Justin, I'm so sorry," Kate sobbed. "I'm sorry for everything. Last summer. And the summer before. And yesterday."

Justin held her tightly and rocked her back and forth. "It's okay, Kate," he said. "It's okay. We're here now. Together. I won't let go of you, I promise."

Kate lifted her head and stared out at the sea. The two small boats were approaching the shore. She could hear the men in them yelling back and forth. Her eyes strayed to the right, to the remains of Justin's boat, *Kate*, capsized and torn.

No more, she couldn't look anymore. Her

eyes fled away to the clear open water. The beautiful blue-green ocean. It would be the last time she saw it. Probably the last thing she'd ever see.

Justin's arms tightened, and she heard a splash, and another. Two of the armed men jumping into the shallow water to pull the boats to shore, she thought. She tried to breath, but she was starting to pant. Mooch was barking again. *They'll just shoot him*, Kate thought suddenly. Justin held her. Her heart was pounding.

"Oh my god," she whispered as she stared at the water. "Oh my god."

She blinked.

"Justin?" she whispered, hardly daring to believe it. "Justin, look. Look!"

Two

Chelsea Lennox and Connor Riordan were standing on the boardwalk in the afternoon sun, she dressed in her bathrobe and he looking totally confused. Chelsea had left work early to go home and confess everything to Connor, but she'd been disappointed to find that he wasn't at home working. Then Antonio had shown up on Grace's doorstep, and that was the last straw. Chelsea couldn't wait any longer. She had to go out and find Connor—and tell him everything.

Chelsea's heart started pounding in her chest. She was about to tell Connor the whole truth about her and Antonio, and she worried that soon he might not be her husband anymore.

"What is it, Chels?" Connor asked. "What could be so important that you ran out of the house in your bathrobe to find me?"

"It's terrible," Chelsea sighed, dropping her head into her hands. "It's terrible, that's what it is."

"What?" Connor asked. "You sound so serious." A smile played at the edges of his mouth. "Don't tell me—you didn't make one of your portraits pretty enough, and they stiffed you the tip? Let's see, you blew a hundred dollars on a new dress and you think I won't like it? No wait, I've got it—you washed my favorite shirt with some Craypas you left in your pocket, and now I'm going to look like I just came back from a van tour with a thousand Deadheads?"

"Connor, stop it!" Chelsea burst out. "Can't you ever stop joking, even for a minute? You're never serious. And when you are, it's only about that novel"—she said "novel" as if she were saying "trash"—"or that Jannah. You can make Jannah laugh all you want, but this isn't a joke. I'm trying to tell you something serious now."

Connor's mouth flattened into a tight line. "Okay, come on. Let's go sit on that bench and talk."

They walked to the nearest empty bench on the boardwalk and sat down. Chelsea was all too aware of the gaping space between them. They might as well be strangers, she thought.

"Look, I'm sorry," Chelsea said, "but you're

not making this easy. I have something serious to talk to you about. Something terrible."

"Well," he said, his voice flat, "how terrible is it then?"

"It's so terrible," Chelsea whispered, her voice failing for a moment, "so terrible that I don't know if our marriage will survive it."

Connor blinked.

This was it. The fateful moment. It was now or never. Tell Connor everything now, and risk divorce, or bury it forever in her heart and risk going mad. Divorce and madness weren't great options, but at lease divorce could give you your dignity back, eventually—even if it did go against the Church.

"I have a confession to make," she said slowly.

"I thought .you did that kind of thing in church," Connor replied.

"Yeah, well, sometimes church isn't enough," Chelsea admitted. "Sometimes you need forgiveness from someone else besides God."

"Forgiveness," Connor repeated woodenly.

"Yes," Chelsea said. "Forgiveness from your husband."

"And what does your husband have to forgive you for?"

"For making a terrible mistake," Chelsea said. "I have to tell you what happened at the christening."

"Something tells me you didn't just drop the baby," Connor said, though the joke fell flat even for him.

Chelsea shook her head. "I didn't even get to hold the baby. It was before that. When I got to Washington, B.D. picked me up at the train station. And he had a friend with him. An old friend." She paused. "His name is Antonio."

"Antonio?" Connor said, searching her face. At the mention of the name, Connor's face tightened. His eyes glazed over, as if he was trying to look into the past, see something he'd maybe missed. "Please don't tell me he's the mistake, Chels."

Chelsea couldn't bring herself to look at him. She kept her eyes on her hands, which she'd clasped tightly together in her lap.

"I knew him when I was younger," Chelsea began. "We spent a lot of time together. He was a . . . a friend of mine, too. Anyway, after I got to Washington, it turned out that we had to go to Pittsburgh to get the christening outfit my grandmother left behind—"

"Your whole family went to Pittsburgh?" Connor asked.

"No. Just me," Chelsea whispered, ready to cry. "And Antonio."

"Just you and Antonio?" Connor said, his face beginning to turn red. "And what happened with you and Antonio?"

"The car broke down," Chelsea whispered, looking up in time to see Connor wince.

"The car broke down," he muttered. "Bloody likely."

"It *did*," Chelsea pleaded. "My mother's old car, and there was only one place to stay. With one room." Chelsea stopped, and Connor was looking at her closely now. "And one bed," she finished softly. "Like a bad movie." She tried to chuckle but the sound was more like choking.

"I'll say like a bad movie. I could have written the script myself."

"And then—" Chelsea closed her eyes because she knew she couldn't look at Connor while she told him.

"Okay, okay," Connor said, steadying himself. "So, it's not that bad, right? I mean, a little flicking of the old eyelashes, a little flirting, a little hand-holding at worst—right? I mean, I can live with a little hand-holding."

But with one look at Chelsea he knew that hand-holding wasn't the worst of it. He sat up straight.

"Chelsea," he said quietly and soberly—as serious as Chelsea had ever seen him. "Whatever's going on with you two, am I going to be able to live with it?"

The tears were forming so quickly in Chelsea's eyes that Connor's face became a blur. "I don't know," she said, biting her lip. She closed her eyes and dove in. "He kissed me."

Connor held up his hands as if fending off a punch. "Thank you, that's just lovely. And it's quite enough. Yes, thank you very much."

"But I have to tell you," Chelsea said, her voice quavering. "I decided it was the only dignified thing to do."

Connor laughed ruefully, clapping his hands on his knees. "Well, Chels, if you want to know the truth, the way you're acting, the way you're talking about this, you probably don't have to say another word. I don't need you to tell me anything else. I've got a vivid imagination. I think I get the picture. And it ain't pretty, as John Wayne would say."

Connor sagged against the bench. Chelsea squinted. Was he crying too? She couldn't tell.

"Okay, so a little kiss," Connor said.

"And then—" Chelsea said quietly.

"And then!" Connor exploded, his fist tight and shaking. "And then! I can't believe you're actually going to tell me what happened next! As if I can't figure it out myself. I think you should be the one to move out, Chelsea, seeing as how my leaving would totally throw off my writing—which, by the way, you don't seem to care about at all. But let's stick to one subject at a time. So—a few days away, and watch out for the mystery man from the past! Is this what happens every time a 'friend' of yours shows up?" Connor was sputtering with anger. "Just tell me one thing," he said. "How long have you wanted to, uh, get together with this Antonio guy?"

Chelsea just sat there, wringing her hands.

"Well?" Connor said angrily, his face reddening, his hands clenching. "Can't you even do me the honor of giving me that piece of information?"

Suddenly Chelsea stopped crying. "I don't know what you're getting so angry about, Connor. It's not like you don't have a past," Chelsea cried. "What about your old girlfriend from Ireland? What about Molly?"

"I don't recall going to a motel with Molly," Connor retorted.

"You didn't have to go to the motel—she was already carrying around a baby!"

"But it wasn't mine!" Connor yelled. "Remember the blood tests? It wasn't mine."

"But it could have been. You *knew* it could have been."

"How can you compare this?" Connor cried. "You and I weren't married then. You're the one who . . . who . . ."

"Well, what about you?" Chelsea lashed out, guilt and shame bolstering her defenses. "You were supposed to be oh-so-busy on your precious book that you couldn't even spend an hour at David's good-bye party or at a concert at the grandstand, let alone a few days to christen *your goddaughter*. If you'd been with me, none of this would have happened. But as soon as I leave, you find all the time in the world to hang out with your new friend, *Jannah Britt*! I'm not the only one around here who's been keeping secrets, or having a fling, or a flirtation, or whatever it was—"

"Don't talk about Jannah like that!" Connor yelled.

"Why?" Chelsea cried. "Do you need to defend her virtue or something? Let's not play games here, Connor. I'm being completely honest, and the least I expect is for you to be perfectly honest too. It's all over. No more secrets. I'm giving you the truth, but I want the truth in return."

Connor whistled and rolled his eyes. "I can't believe this. It's like a movie—"

"This isn't a movie, Connor!" Chelsea cried. "This is real life. Real . . . life! Maybe that's been the problem. Maybe you're so wrapped up in your little fictional world all the time, writing that book of yours, and talking about writing books with Jannah and your little writing group, you've lost track of reality."

"Jannah likes my company," Connor snapped.

"She laughs at my jokes. She thinks I have talent. She cares about my book."

"Antonio cares about me, too!" Chelsea cried, unsure exactly why she was defending him.

"Jannah knew I was sad. And she wanted me to stay," Connor continued.

"Antonio wanted to kiss me. And I wanted him to," Chelsea said forlornly. There. She'd said it, but she sure didn't feel free.

"Well, as long as you wanted to," Connor sneered. "I guess that makes it okay. And just for your information, I *wanted* to be with Jannah, as well."

At his words, Chelsea's eyes welled with tears, and she covered her face with her hands. It had been one thing to imagine, but quite another to hear.

"I can't believe you!" she cried. "You're saying you did it!"

"You mean that *you* did it!" Connor cried.

"You slept with her," Chelsea mumbled, eyes wet.

"You slept with him." Connor shook his head, stunned.

"Don't worry, Connor," she choked. "I'm leaving tonight. I'll go back to Grace's."

Connor just shook his head, totally dazed. He gazed into Chelsea's rich black eyes. "How did we get here, Chels? I mean, just a few weeks ago we were happily married. We were poor, but happily married. Then I got that letter from the publishers, and *whammo*, everything fell apart overnight." Connor breathed, cradling his head in his hands, his fingers in his flaming hair. "This marriage is in serious jeopardy," he said.

"No," Chelsea corrected, though the words cut through her like a knife. She rose and started walking home, hugging her arms tightly across her chest. "No, Connor," she whispered shakily. "This marriage is over."

THREE

When Grace Caywood remembered what she'd told her friend Marta about being "off men" for a couple of years, she had to laugh. A couple of weeks was more like it, which was exactly how long it had taken Grace to admit that not only was she *not* "off men" in general, but there were already two men she might be interested in.

True, neither of them was David Jacobs, the love of her life, who was probably at that very moment flying his F-15 somewhere over Taiwan. Grace missed him. Badly. But she also knew that she might never see him again. When he left, they couldn't afford to make any promises to each other.

David was a one-of-a-kind guy. Smart, wise, sensitive, handsome, *and* older. Grace had figured on mourning him for a long time before anyone else would look even half as interesting to her. But, as they say, life works in mysterious ways.

The amazing thing, Grace thought as she glanced back and forth between Carr and Wilton, was that she could be attracted to two so completely different guys. And they just happened to be standing together in her kitchen.

Grace had been so busy making phone calls, she hadn't even showered or dressed yet. But here was Wilton, asking her on a date, and Carr, freshly showered after a day of lifeguarding. Grace noticed that he was smiling smugly at Wilton. She wished more than anything that she could just disappear.

"So, what do you say, Grace?" Wilton said, snapping Grace out of a daze. "Do you want to come over tonight and watch the *F-Troop* marathon?"

F-Troop was Wilton Groves's *only* anti-intellectual obsession, as far as Grace could tell. He was quirky and bookish, the most serious person Grace had ever met. Wilton was so out of the ordinary for Ocean City, and for that matter the world, that Grace sometimes wondered what passing spaceship had dropped him here. The idea of finding him even vaguely interesting, *as a man*, was almost a joke. His face was cute enough, in an intellectual kind of way, but his body was on the skinny, undeveloped side. Physically, he was not the type that Grace had ever found attractive or sexy.

But it was true that after Wilton's first day on the job at one of Grace's beach stands, when he forgot to make the cash deposits at the bank and Grace had gone to his condo to get them, she'd had a pretty good time hanging out with him and watching *F-Troop. F-Troop*, of all things. And then the other day she'd spent the afternoon talking to him on the beach. It was funny, and a little embarrassing to admit, but Grace enjoyed talking with Wilton. There was something nice about being seen as a *person* and not just a *body*.

"*F-Troop*," Carr said. "Sounds like a good time."

Grace glanced at Carr, and he grinned at her, trying to stifle a laugh. That grin works wonders, Grace thought. Carr Savett was quite possibly the most handsome man Grace had ever seen.

"Grace?" Wilton's voice reminded her that he was still there. "Did you hear me?"

"Hmmm." She nodded, still marveling at the blueness of Carr's eyes.

"So. Would you like to come over? We can watch TV and then maybe . . . hang out . . . and talk."

Smiling at Carr, Grace was about to say no to Wilton when she paused. Though she felt pretty sure that Carr was going to ask her to go out, she didn't actually have a date with him yet. Surprisingly, she found herself considering Wilton's offer.

"Grace?" Wilton prompted.

Suddenly the phone rang.

Grace was so startled, she snatched up the receiver on the first ring. "Hello," she said.

"I'm calling for Carr," a shrill, high voice cried out.

"Who's calling, please?" Grace asked, though she had a strong hunch she knew who it was.

"Who's this?" the voice whined. "This is Jody, and I need to speak to Carr—now. It's important."

"Are you calling from work?" Grace asked sweetly, looking back at Carr as he slouched against the wall, eyeing her. He had no idea who was on the phone, and that was fine with Grace. She knew by now that Jody was his girlfriend from home. And Grace had already heard too many of Carr's defensive, apologetic, one-sided conversations.

"What does it matter to you?" Jody screeched. "I need to speak to Carr—please put him on the phone."

Poor Carr, Grace thought, her eyes traveling slowly up and down his body, bringing a deep red blush to his face. He didn't really deserve this, did he? Thanks to Jody, Grace had just made up her mind.

"That's just fine," Grace said smoothly, "and thanks for calling. I appreciate your looking into this for me. I'll let you know what I decide."

She hung up the phone, abruptly cutting off the whiny, high-pitched voice.

"Just a business call," Grace said, smiling at Carr, then Wilton. "Listen, Wilton, I really appreciate the invitation, but I have plans tonight. Remember Marta? You almost met her at that party I had."

"Yes, I remember her. You told me not to bother, that she was moving out."

"She did move out," Grace explained, "and I've been dying to see her new place. We sort of had tentative plans for tonight, and she just called to tell me she was settled in enough to have company. So I'm going over there. But, really, thanks for inviting me, Wilton." Grace felt a little uncomfortable about lying to him so easily.

"Sure," he answered tonelessly.

"Some other time, okay?" Grace pressed, feeling more guilty than she thought she would.

"Yeah, sure, Grace," Wilton said softly, trying to hide his disappointment. "Some other time. See you."

Wilton left, and Grace sighed heavily as the screen door banged shut behind him.

"So," Carr said. "Do you really have to go to Marta's tonight? Or would you like to go out with me?"

"Well, I suppose I could postpone with Marta," Grace said coyly. "If you can make me a better offer."

Just then the phone started to ring, and Carr instinctively reached for it. Grace put out her hand and stopped him.

"Let it ring," Grace said. "If it's important, they'll call back." It was definitely Jody, Grace thought. No need for Carr to be reminded of her at this very moment.

Grace still felt badly about blowing off Wilton, but when she looked into Carr's eyes, the bad feeling melted away. A new feeling—excitement—started coiling in her stomach. They stood staring deeply at each other until the loud, insistent ringing finally stopped.

"Hurry up and get dressed," Carr said finally. "And I'll show you what I had in mind."

FOUR

"Is that what I think it is?" Kate shouted, pulling herself from Justin's grasp and frantically waving her arms in the air.

Justin turned to watch her antics, shaking his head in wonder, until he followed her gaze out to sea. Around the southern point of their small barrier island came the distinctive white prow of a United States Coast Guard cutter.

"Don't tell me you can't see that!" Kate shouted to Allegra. Allegra had never admitted that her glasses had been fake, though she hadn't had any trouble seeing since she lost them. Besides, Kate herself had tried them out and knew they were just plain old glass lenses. Still, she liked to comment on Allegra's mysterious vision problem whenever she got the chance.

Allegra turned and looked past them to where the Coast Guard cutter was coming into full view. For a moment she had the strangest look on her face. Kate wasn't sure, but it seemed like a mixture of disbelief and, of all things, fear. Kate was about to ask what in the world Allegra had to fear from the Coast Guard when Allegra gathered her wits and broke out into a happy grin.

Then Justin came up behind Kate and swooped her into his embrace, spinning her around until they almost fell onto the beach.

"Oh, Kate, baby, we're okay," he crooned as he dipped his head down to kiss her. He squeezed her tightly before he stepped away and turned to smile at Allegra. But before Justin had even steadied himself, Allegra launched herself into his arms.

"We're safe!" she cried jubilantly, throwing her arms around Justin's neck as though he'd no doubt been planning to give *her* a relieved spin around the beach too. Allegra reached up and tangled her hands in his hair and pulled him down for a loud kiss. Startled, Justin practically pushed her over trying to get away, but Allegra ignored it.

"They must have been following Chernak," she surmised happily. Kate couldn't help but wonder if Allegra's face was flushed from relief, or from the close contact with Justin.

"Well, it sure wasn't the signal fire you *didn't* light that led them here," she snapped, fuming at the way Allegra never seemed to miss an opportunity to get physical with her boyfriend.

Two loud, sharp horn blasts from the cutter startled them all, and they spun toward the water. Finally Chernak had seen the boat. Men were scurrying all over the deck, tossing their machine guns down left and right. The two small outboards were almost ashore; four men stood by them in water up to their thighs, their faces staring in shock at the cutter as it came into full view.

"Drop your weapons," came the calm, commanding voice of the Coast Guard captain, blasting from a speaker mounted above the cutter's control booth. "Stop what you are doing and remain with your hands above your head. Prepare to be boarded. You, on the island. Drop your weapons and await instruction."

"Is he talking to us?" Kate asked, confused.

"He must mean those guys almost on the beach," Justin whispered back.

In moments two small boats sped away from the cutter; one toward Chernak's white sailboat, and the other toward the island. Justin, Kate, and Allegra watched as Chernak was led, unarmed, onto the small launch and brought back to the cutter.

Two men leaped out of the second launch, waving their pistols, and started barking orders at Chernak's henchmen. Four others pulled the launch to shore and came steadily toward them.

Kate was smiling, until she glanced over at Allegra. Her eyes were slits, her mouth a grim, determined line.

"Are we glad to see you," Justin sighed, about to step forward. In a split second they were surrounded. Kate wasn't sure what was going on, but there was no mistaking the fact that none of the faces around them looked at all friendly.

"Wait a minute," Kate cried, as one of the Coast Guard officers pulled her roughly away from Justin.

Automatically, Justin stepped after her, his arm out to protect her. Before Kate could blink, there were four guns leveled at him, and he froze.

"I don't think you understand what's going on here," Justin whispered.

"Oh, I think we do," one of the guards replied. "The formal term is drug trafficking. Which in some states, pal, depending on the size of the stash, carries a life sentence."

FIVE

The music at Floaters, the lifeguard hang-out, was loud and fast—fast enough to keep Grace sweating and smiling without the aid of a drink. It was still hard to really go out in O.C. without drinking at all, but being with Carr certainly helped.

Grace could *almost* get high just looking at him. He looked as though he'd just stepped out of an advertisement for Banana Republic, or the Gap, with his blond hair falling rakishly across his forehead, and his incredible cheekbones, and startling blue eyes. And Grace wasn't the only woman who thought so.

According to her tally, Grace was sporting a few hundred imaginary daggers in her bare back.

Not only was Carr in great shape, but he didn't seem to be too interested in drinking either.

Apparently it went along with the "keep your body beautiful" campaign he'd been pushing on her lately.

"Don't you drink?" Grace had asked when they'd gone to the bar and Carr had ordered a soda.

"Oh, my friends and I drink beers back in Kansas," he'd admitted, "but not much else. I'm not legal here anyway."

"No," Grace agreed. "Not legal, exactly, but in this town it doesn't take much effort to get around that."

Carr shrugged. "Why take the chance? Anyway, alcohol is terrible for your body. And I like to stay in control of myself."

So, Grace thought, he doesn't want to do anything he'll regret later. Obviously Carr was still thinking about Jody, and he wasn't ready to go crazy on his new run for independence. Grace couldn't really fault him for it—even if every time she looked at him she wondered what it would be like to kiss him.

Grace had dated a lot of very good-looking men in her time. Justin, for starters, who back in high school could always gather a crowd by standing still anywhere for just a few minutes. And David, of course, who had an incredibly sexy, tall-and-dark look. But Carr was different. He was almost unnatural. Grace noticed that even men couldn't help themselves from staring at him.

Well, if he wasn't ready to kiss her just yet, that was fine. She was willing to wait. Grace figured the end of the night was just long enough.

They were out on the floor, jammed close together in the throng of stripped-down, sweaty dancers. The music was fantastic—Smashing Pumpkins, Nine Inch Nails, Red Hot Chili Peppers. And then, of course, the occasional throwback—Eric Clapton, an old U2 song. The crowd loved it.

Grace could see some mosh dancing starting back near the bathrooms. She was finding less and less space for herself as the pit began to grow. Carr didn't have much choice but to press up against her—it was that or be swallowed by five women near him that he *hadn't* come with. His hands, with nowhere else to go but his own pockets, came to rest lightly on her gyrating hips.

"Are you okay out here?" Grace yelled in the direction of his ear.

"Sure," he replied. "As long as you are."

He was lying. Grace could see he was uncomfortable, partially from the crush of bodies but mostly from the crush of *her* body. Grace enjoyed the dancing, but she couldn't help feeling sorry for Carr. He was trying so hard not to let his fingers slip off her hips and onto the bare skin of her lower back.

"Let's find a table and sit," she suggested. "Better yet, let's go out for a walk and get some air."

At the mention of air, Carr brightened.

They had to shove their way through the pulsing crowd. Grace felt quite a few stray hands brush along her spine.

"Sneaky perverts!" she yelled out around her, knowing her voice was drowned by the blaring music. Thank god she was following the blond Man of Steel, or she'd never get out.

"Must have been all the cows you herded!" Grace teased, holding onto one of Carr's arms and feeling it flex below her fingers.

"Excuse me?" Carr asked as they practically fell out of the packed doorway onto the sandy beach.

"I said," Grace repeated, giving his biceps a squeeze, "it must have been all the cows you herded that made you this strong."

"I didn't herd cows in Kansas, Grace," Carr replied easily. "I worked at the granary, lifting enormous sacks of barley and corn."

"Well, I *knew* muscles didn't grow like that by themselves," Grace crowed.

"And I *did* drink a lot of milk," Carr continued. "Milk makes a body strong. Did you know that?"

"I think I might have heard something like that on TV once or twice," Grace replied.

"Well, it's true. Especially for women. Women should drink a lot of milk, or they'll shrink up when they're older. It'd be much better for you than all that Diet Coke you poison yourself with."

"Thanks, Carr," Grace said dryly, taking his arm and pulling him in the direction of the beach. "Let's leave the Kansas health report for a while, shall we? I'm not Dorothy, and I don't really want to go home yet."

Grace slipped off her shoes and carried them in one hand. The sun had set a few hours ago, and the sky was a deep dark blue. A chunk of the moon hung over the ocean, making the waves glow as they rolled into shore. The line of empty white lifeguard stands stood out against the dark night air in a long procession up the beach. They looked smaller when there were no people on the beach to measure them against.

"So how's lifeguarding been?" Grace asked teasingly. "Everything you ever imagined?"

"Oh, it's great," Carr said. "By the way, there's some guy, Justin Garrett? He's a friend of yours, right?"

"Yup," Grace said. "We both grew up here. The lucky local yokels."

"You know, I hear about him a lot," Carr continued. "Where is he now, anyway?"

"Somewhere in the Atlantic Ocean, I guess."

"You mean he's dead?" Carr asked quickly.

"No," Grace said. "Although it's not a new thought when it comes to Justin. I meant he's somewhere in the Atlantic on his boat. With Kate. She's his girlfriend, and an ex-roommate of mine. They're sailing his boat back here from the Bahamas."

"So he is coming back to Ocean City?" Carr pressed.

"Sure," Grace replied. "In a few weeks or so."

"A few weeks? Will Kate live with you again? Does that mean Justin will move in too?" Carr asked pointedly.

"I really don't know, Carr," Grace said, exasperated. "They'll be back when they're back, and I guess, sure, if they want to, they can move back in. Kate had the other big bedroom on the top floor, and she knows there's enough room for two. She already tried it once."

"With Justin?"

"No. With some other guy. The *last time* we thought Justin was dead."

"Do you think they're going to try lifeguarding again?" Carr asked, looking out at the sea as they walked.

"I don't know, Carr," Grace said a little angrily.

"They're my *friends*, not my children. And even if they were my children, I wouldn't profess to know their plans. Okay?"

Carr shrugged. "Okay. Just asking." They walked a little farther in silence.

"If he moves in with you, where do you think he'll keep his boat?"

"Carr!" Grace gave him a steely gaze.

"Just curious," he said. "You've got a great house, but you don't have a dock. I just wonder what everyone does with their boats."

"That's probably what the marina is for," Grace pointed out.

"Right," Carr agreed. "That would make sense." He smiled and shook his head. "I love this place. It's so amazing."

"You mean Ocean City?" Grace asked wondrously.

"When I was growing up, people talked about what the city was like," Carr explained. "But I never imagined it like this. It's so . . . busy and full. Everyone has something to do—"

"Yeah," Grace added wryly, "like go to the beach. Big plans."

"And there's so many different kinds of people here. You know," Carr said softly, "the other day I was walking back from work, and I saw cars pass me with license plates from *eight different states*, if you can believe it. Back home I didn't see people from eight different *counties* except once a year at the state fair."

"That's pretty amazing," Grace said, cocking her head.

Carr nodded. "I think so. This place has changed my whole life."

"Ocean City?" Grace checked again, just to make sure they really were talking about the same place.

"Yup." Carr nodded. "I might never be able to leave."

"That's funny," Grace said. "I used to go to the airport all the time to watch the planes take off. That's how badly I wanted to get out of here."

"Why would you want to leave?" Carr asked.

Grace thought of her trip to New York City last summer, and all the months she'd spent with Justin at sea—crossing the Atlantic, sailing around the Mediterranean, all the countries she'd visited, the museums, the history. All those places had made her feel so small for sitting around at home doing nothing, knowing nothing. She'd been so eager for more. She still was. She probably always would be.

"I don't know if I can explain it," she answered. "There's just so many other things to do in the world. So many other places to be besides Ocean City. It's my home, but it's not the end of the world."

Carr shrugged his perfect shoulders and smiled. "I guess not. But to me this place is fine. A lot better than Kansas," he said quickly. He blushed, and Grace realized he was probably thinking of Jody and feeling guilty again.

Grace nodded. "I guess it is."

No sense in being disappointed, Grace figured. Carr wasn't a mental giant, but then again, probably the only person in the world who really knew what she meant was David. He felt the same way as her. That was why he wasn't *in* Ocean City anymore.

Grace sighed. Carr was gorgeous, but there just weren't many men like David in the world—handsome *and* smart.

The only times lately that Grace had come close to having conversations like the ones she'd had with David was when she was with Wilton. Wilton was definitely smart. Talking with him was exciting in its own way, a different kind of challenge.

Grace felt Carr shyly take her hand. His long fingers twined with hers, and she felt the shock of physical awareness travel through her. She realized she was still unsettled about how she'd lied to Wilton, but she pushed the thought away. A breeze ruffled Carr's hair, and Grace had to catch her breath. Now just wasn't the time for feeling sorry. And anyway, with

Carr's looks, he didn't need to say much at all to keep her interested.

"It's been a nice night, hasn't it," Carr said awkwardly, as they approached the house from the beach.

"Sure it has," Grace agreed. "Although it's not over yet. And look, we've already made it to our backyard."

It was amazing to Grace how comfortable she was in O.C. sometimes. Even with her wistful thoughts, this part of the beach was her backyard after all, and she felt a bit proprietary of it. Sometimes, when she stood on her sun deck watching people on the sand, she wished she could send them away—as if throwing a Frisbee twenty feet from her house could count as trespassing.

She'd worked hard to get this house, she thought. Well, lived through enough, anyway.

As much as they'd seemed to hate each other, Grace wasn't happy that her mother had died. It wasn't the nicest way to inherit a house and financial security.

And Grace was working hard now. She really wanted to make this home happier than the one she'd grown up in.

The house that Grace built, she said to herself, chuckling. A house for her family; for Bo and for Roan. It was only a piece of paper that made Grace Roan's legal guardian. But at the rate Bo and Roan were going, it was likely that Roan would still be a part of Grace's family even after she turned eighteen. Perhaps someday they really would be sisters. As disgusting as Bo and Roan's sickly-sweet love life was, Grace had to admit that the idea of having a sister was appealing. And then there were all her friends she'd taken in at different times. She had made herself into quite the den mother, hadn't she?

"It's really a great place," Carr said, following her gaze to the huge, inviting house behind them. "I am the luckiest guy in Ocean City, I think. First I get a great job with the beach patrol, and then an even better landlord."

Grace smiled at the compliment. Correction, she wasn't a "den mother" to everybody. And she certainly didn't feel motherly when she looked at Carr, though it was hard to look at Carr at all and not wish to populate the world with little clones. He could probably sell his genes on the stock market. They'd set a standard higher than gold.

"What are you thinking about?" Carr murmured.

"Don't ask," Grace laughed. "You don't want to scare yourself. Come on, let's go in and raid the fridge, then sit down and get off our feet. The best dates end that way."

"Raiding the fridge?" Carr asked.

"No, dummy," Grace smirked, pinching his arm hard before she ran away, "getting off your feet!"

Though she'd caught him by surprise and had a head start of about twenty yards, it didn't last very long. They both knew the hundred-yard dash was Grace's maximum effort, and when Carr caught up to her as she was slogging her way around the side of the house, he neatly swept her into his arms and jogged the rest of the way to the front door.

"Home sweet home," Grace panted, trying to catch her breath. "You've got to admit it was a worthy effort."

"Not really," Carr replied seriously. "But if you'd exercise with me like I offered—"

"Don't start in on that again," she said, wondering again how someone could so consistently miss sarcasm when it was aimed at him. Even Wilton knew a joke when he heard one.

Carr held her a few minutes longer than necessary, and finally set her on her feet when they got inside.

"We both know you like me just the way I am," Grace pointed out sweetly, satisfied when she saw the blush on his face.

She leaned sideways against the front door and placed Carr's hands on her hips.

"Don't we?" she pressed, lifting her own hands to his strong, muscled shoulders. *Too bad the beach flock doesn't know what it's missing*, she thought as she tugged Carr toward her. Grace could feel Carr's quickened breathing and the pounding in his chest. She was about to find out if those perfectly formed lips were more than just for show.

She felt his breath on her cheek, and a moment of hesitation. Sorry, Jody, Grace thought. But you're not here. And I am.

Just as their lips were about to meet, there was a loud, sharp thumping that was like an explosion in Grace's head. She shrieked, and Carr jumped away from her.

"I'm sorry . . ." he started to sputter, "I thought—"

"No, no," Grace shook her head. "It's not you."

Someone was hammering on the front door right where Grace's head had been resting.

"Who the hell is that!" Grace cried. Her heart was pounding with shock. Her head was ringing as though a bomb had gone off in her ear. Carr put his hand out against her and pushed her from the front door.

"Stand back. Let me see who it is," he said quickly.

"Okay, Conan." Grace rolled her eyes.

Carr put his foot against the door and opened

it a crack. The next moment he was thrown back against the wall as Chelsea came barreling past him, sobbing hysterically and dragging what looked like a laundry bag behind her.

"Chelsea?" Grace asked, looking at her in confusion. "Chelsea honey, is something wrong with your washing machine? Are you sure it can't wait until morning?"

Chelsea stopped in the foyer and stood still, trying to get her sobbing under control. She shook her heard.

"Okay," Grace said, "it can't wait. Something's wrong?"

Chelsea nodded, and sniffed.

"Do you need to talk?" Grace asked.

Chelsea nodded again.

Grace turned to Carr and shrugged. "There goes the big kiss, frog prince. You won't become a man tonight."

"What?" he said, eyes huge.

"A joke, Carr," Grace explained. "Just a joke. Listen, thanks for a great evening. I had a lot of fun. Now I have to go upstairs, where I may not have very much fun. I'll see you in the morning."

"Okay," Carr said dejectedly. "Good night."

Grace grabbed the laundry bag in one hand and took Chelsea's arm in the other.

"Wanna sleep over?" Grace asked softly. "Follow me, I know just the place for sob stories."

SIX

"So?" Grace asked after she'd settled herself and Chelsea onto her big bed. "Are you going to tell me why you're barging into my house in the middle of the night dragging a laundry bag behind you? It must have been some nightmare. Was it Tide rolling in to drown you or Bounce throwing you around your living room? And it'd better be good," Grace smiled wryly. "You just cost me a kiss I worked for all night."

Chelsea sighed, and blew her nose again. "It was just the fastest way to pack," she said softly, staring at the brightly striped canvas bag at her feet. "Actually, I had all night to pack, but I made some calls and straightened up a bit. I guess I was stalling, hoping Connor would come home, but he didn't."

"So where are you going?" Grace asked.

"Here," Chelsea sniffed. "That is, if you'll let me."

"You're really moving out?" Grace said sadly.

"I think so," Chelsea nodded.

"What happened this time?"

"I told him about Antonio," she said meekly.

"The guy from the christening? You told him about only one room in the motel?" Grace cried. "Chelsea, of course that's going to make him nuts. Why tell him when nothing happened?"

"Because," Chelsea said softly. "I didn't tell you before, but more than nothing happened."

That stopped Grace cold. She looked at Chelsea closely. Before David, Grace hadn't ever held monogamous relationships in high regard. She'd never even had any scruples about stealing someone else's boyfriend.

And look at her now. She was going after Carr, wasn't she? And he had a girlfriend. Even if Carr and Jody were destined to fail, Jody didn't know it yet. And Grace was helping bring it about. She shook her head. But this wasn't about her and Carr. Neither of them were married, and Chelsea was. That's what made Chelsea's news difficult.

"I think," Grace said slowly, "that I don't know what to say."

"I didn't actually sleep with him," Chelsea said, starting to cry again, "if that's what you're thinking."

"Well, okay. If you didn't sleep with him, what's the problem?" Grace asked. "It can't be that bad."

"We kissed," Chelsea admitted.

"In the motel room?" Grace asked.

"Next to the bed. But that was all. Then." Chelsea sighed. "I saw him again. Today."

"Here?" Grace asked. "In Ocean City?"

"He followed me. He wanted to talk. He says—" She gulped. "He says he loves me. That he's always loved me. And—"

"And?" Grace asked.

Chelsea nodded.

"So you . . . did sleep with him?" Grace said softly.

"No!" Chelsea cried, shaking her head. "No, I didn't. But we kissed. Again. Only I pushed him away because I just couldn't—you know, I couldn't. I mean, I love Connor!" Now Chelsea was sobbing again, trying to catch her breath. "I really love him. And he's my husband! But he won't be anymore, we're going to get a divorce I think, because I told him—"

"What exactly did you tell him?" Grace asked. "And for that matter, why tell him anything? You know now that you really love him, Chelsea. So why make him think about what you did or didn't do?"

"The problem isn't what I did or didn't do." Chelsea shook, her voice cracking. "The problem now is what *Connor* did or didn't do." Chelsea looked up with tears in her eyes. "And he *did*!" she wailed mournfully.

It was late, well past midnight, when Chelsea found herself pacing the living room in the dark. Everyone was asleep, and she could practically feel the house's bigness in her bones. She could almost hear the silent chorus of deep, comfortable, restful breathing all around her. It was deafening.

Meanwhile, she'd practically burned a path through the floor from the refrigerator in the kitchen to the telephone in the living room, making laps around various pieces of furniture, opening a window, deciding she was cold, closing it. The clock's ticking echoed in her brain. Outside, she could hear the water rolling up onto the beach. From far off, she heard the braying of a foghorn.

Everything reminded her that time was passing, and that every minute that went by was another minute in the trash can: another minute she was not with Connor, or Antonio. Another minute that Connor was probably with Jannah Britt, laying his head on her experienced writerly shoulders for support—while she was here alone, eating everything in the house that wasn't tied down.

For the fiftieth time that night, she picked up the phone and dialed the first six digits of Antonio's number, then dropped the receiver in its cradle.

Whatever was happening between her and Connor—and what was happening? she wondered—she knew that calling Antonio would only give him the opening he needed to convince her to come over to his motel room. And once she was actually in the room, there was no telling what might happen.

But it wasn't right. If she knew anything about this situation, it was that. She had to stay focused. She wouldn't even set the match to that fire until she figured out what to do with Connor.

"Yeah, but what about him?" she moaned. She didn't even have to close her eyes to imagine the picture: Connor sitting on Jannah's couch, drinking a beer, talking nonchalantly about Chelsea, like she was some lost lover of long ago. And Jannah, of course, was nodding knowingly, rubbing his shoulders for support.

"Come here, Connor," Chelsea heard Jannah say as clearly as if she were in the room. "Why don't you rest your head in my lap and relax. Shhh. Don't think about a thing. Don't worry about a thing. There's only you and me in this room, and the world out there—well, it can take care of itself. . . ."

Of course, the scalp massage did not progress more than two minutes before Jannah bent her head over Connor's and began massaging his gums. Then off went the clothes, flying across the room: shoes, shirts, and shorts strewn over the floor like enormous limp leaves. And Jannah's long, experienced fingers on his body.

Chelsea couldn't bear it. She could practically hear the moaning. The things Connor used to say to her—*only* to her.

Chelsea sat up and pricked up her ears. What was that they were saying? *I love you?*

She lifted a throw pillow and heaved it across the room, where it landed with a thud amid all the other pillows she'd thrown over the course of the night. She gritted her teeth. She was blind with rage.

And no doubt all of it was "research" for their writing. After all, writers needed experience, didn't they? They needed to taste the world. How else were they supposed to write about it? All of it was forgivable. After all, were they not artistes?

"Yeah, but you're a human being first!" she cried out at the empty walls.

* * *

Across the street, Connor sat at his writing desk in the dark. He could feel the pages of his novel under his hands, his borrowed laptop computer sitting in front of him. But he couldn't do a thing. He almost hated his half-finished book.

He swiped at it, and a few pages whipped into the dark all over the floor.

How could he have let it get between him and Chelsea? Who was this Antonio guy, anyway? Part of Connor doubted that Chelsea was telling him the whole truth. Sure, they'd had their problems, but for her to suddenly go off one weekend and return saying she slept with the guy? It was almost too much to believe.

Connor shook his head. He'd never have thought her conscience would let her.

"Well, just goes to show you, old boy," he said to himself. "Just because you marry a woman doesn't mean you know her."

Connor whipped around. He thought he'd heard something, the shuffling of feet, maybe. Suddenly, before him, out of the dark, materialized Chelsea on someone's arm, heading through a doorway leading to a bedroom. He could see Chelsea tilt her head back, her lips part. He saw this stranger's hands working Chelsea's shoulders . . . lower . . . down to the small of her back.

"Damn it all!" Connor cried, kicking his feet,

sending one shoe, then the other, at the window. Of course, he missed, and the shoes landed with a double thud on the floor.

The phone rang.

He propped up his head and peered into the dark of the living room. But he was glued to his seat. He didn't want to talk to anybody, unless it was Chelsea, unless she was calling to say she was coming back to him. But it wouldn't be her. She was "otherwise occupied," Connor was sure. After all, he'd seen it with his own eyes.

The phone kept ringing, and Connor half stood. Suddenly he thought it might be Jannah.

Just her name brought a small smile to his face. He pictured her soft, wavy hair, her long fingers, that blinding grin; and, most importantly, her sympathetic and talented ear. He liked her, that was for sure. He had to admit, Chelsea was pretty perceptive to have picked it up: There was a part of him that needed what only Jannah seemed to be able to give. He liked that she was older, and he liked most that she was a writer and understood perfectly the needs of a writer, no matter how ridiculous they seemed.

More than once he'd fantasized a life with her, each of them in their own rooms in Jannah's condo, rapping away at their keyboards, producing brilliant prose, bringing each other cups of coffee for a little break, reading to each other little passages they'd just finished . . . a midday rendezvous on the living-room couch for lunch . . . a rewarding, celebratory beer on the boardwalk after a long, hard day of writing. . . .

Though wasn't it Jannah herself who'd said that it was one thing for two writers to have a little—how had she put it?—liaison, but that no city, much less any apartment, would be big enough to contain the ambitions and needs of two married writers. It'd be stormy going, she'd said. They'd probably end up dead in each other's arms. Tragic, yes, but not really conducive to getting a lot of work done.

"Jannah," Connor said, as if trying the word out on his tongue. "Jannah and Connor."

Connor bolted for the phone, but by the time he reached it, there was nothing but dial tone.

He collapsed into the couch. "Jannah," he said. "Jan—"

He couldn't finish. He peered at the closed front door. "Chelsea," he moaned. "Chelsea, I love you."

He sat forward, resting his elbows on his knees and letting his head drop into his hands. "What's the point? What's the bloody point?" he said over and over.

SEVEN

"Now, let me get this straight," the captain said carefully to Kate, Justin, and Allegra, his head cocked and a look of disbelief in his cool gray eyes. "You want me to believe that you had *no idea* the drugs were even on your boat?"

He seemed too young to be a captain in the Coast Guard, Kate thought, watching him nervously. Probably just thirty or so. But if dead seriousness and suspicion counted for anything, he'd probably gotten his share of commendations. He was actually quite handsome, with close-cut jet-black hair. And he probably had a friendly face when he chose to show it. Only at this particular moment, he wasn't showing it to them.

"Of course I had no idea," Justin explained again, both palms flat on the table in front of him. "I just got back down to the boat a few weeks ago—well after all the work had been done on it. I was concerned that something had been done to my boat without my permission, and I had to question a lot of people before I finally got Trevor Chernak's name from anyone."

As if on cue, everyone in the room turned to look at Chernak, leaning against a wall to keep his white suit unwrinkled. He looked calm and unruffled, though he was flanked by armed guards. Kate, Justin, and Allegra were sitting at a table with the captain.

"He brought us to his house and told us he'd done the repairs because he'd heard that Justin had drowned in a boating accident," Kate explained. "He said he was doing it as a kind of remembrance, or something. As a gift."

"And that's exactly the truth, my dear captain," Chernak added from his spot on the wall. "I had no idea who was coming for the boat, or indeed, if anyone ever would. I was quite happy to see that it was the fellow himself."

"If I want to hear from you, I'll let you know." The captain glared at him. "Until then, save your story. Go on," he said to Justin.

"Well, there's not much else except what we told you. When we found the drugs after we crashed, we got rid of them."

The captain's face remained expressionless.

"We cut the bags open under water," Justin said.

Kate glanced at Chernak and saw him discreetly roll his eyes. *He doesn't believe us!* she thought, amazed. *What does he think we are, smugglers?*

Just then a man rushed into the room in a sleek black diving suit. He'd obviously just come out of the water. He stopped inside the doorway, and instantly a small puddle began forming at his feet.

"Captain," he said, saluting smartly.

The captain nodded curtly. "Go on."

"It's like they said, sir. Damaged keel, a well-insulated compartment. But nothing there. Except a lot of ripped up empty plastic bags caught in the wreckage."

Kate was watching Chernak. His eyes bulged in shock. Then he glanced at her, and his eyes locked on to hers. Fury was all she could see in them at first, and then she saw the unspoken threat. A shiver ran down her spine.

In an instant Chernak had schooled his features back into a blank stare, and looked away. His slow gaze settled on Allegra, and Kate saw his eyes squint dubiously. And curiously.

"Thank you, Ensign. That will be all."

The captain turned to them and, for the first time, offered an apologetic smile.

"Well, I'm sorry for what you had to go through," he said politely. "It's procedure, of course. We've been after our friend here for quite a while." He nodded in Chernak's direction.

"If you've wanted to see me, you've always had an open invitation to my home," Chernak said slowly. "Of course, you already know that. You just don't seem to want to take me up on my hospitality."

"Hospitality?" Allegra muttered. "Yeah, right."

The captain looked at her in surprise. "And I take it you know Mr. Chernak as well?"

Allegra glanced up quickly. "Oh. Well. Yes," she admitted. "Yes, I do." She looked into the captain's eyes, and Kate saw her gaze soften. "I met him under some rather . . . unfortunate circumstances. And I can't say it was a happy association. I'm rather embarrassed to have to talk about it with him here—"

"Oh, Allegra darling," Chernak interrupted. "You were never one to be embarrassed, my dear heart. Please. You underestimate yourself—"

"Stop!" Allegra cried, throwing her hands to her ears and looking at the captain. "Really, there's nothing to be done about it, not in any legal way of course, but please, must I stay here and listen . . . to those filthy lies." She started to sob. "I'm just not that way. . . ."

"Get him out of here!" the captain barked immediately, and the two guards jerked Chernak from the wall.

"Allegra *dear,*" Chernak hissed quickly as they pulled him away, "we both know what *way* you are, and when we see each other again—" The door closed swiftly behind him.

Kate was surprised to see the way Allegra broke down. *She must be serious*, Kate thought. *No one could fake that kind of reaction. I still don't trust her, but maybe she's been telling the truth about Chernak.* Kate caught Justin's eye, and they looked at each other guiltily.

"I'm just . . . so relieved, now . . ." Allegra managed through her sobs, "that he won't . . . be able to terrorize . . . anyone else. Thank God he's finally going to jail . . . for something."

"Jail?" the captain said. "Oh, I'm sorry. I see that you don't understand. This might be hard to believe," the captain sighed, "but we've got to let him go."

Allegra's head shot up. In an instant her tears were gone. "What do you mean?" she snapped. "How can you let him go?"

Everyone's jaw dropped, including the handsome captain. His gray eyes turned hard in a manner of seconds. Kate could see Allegra make an effort to pull herself together. The anger disappeared from her face as though she'd pulled down a shade in a window. Suddenly her eyes were moist again, and her lower lip trembled.

"I mean," she said softly, her voice cracking, "how can you let him go after all this? Drug smuggling? He was coming onto the beach with weapons!" She wiped her eyes. "Don't you think he would have used them? I . . . know him well enough . . . to know that, at least." One of the crew had given her a shirt to wear when they were brought aboard, and Allegra ran her hands down the front of it to smooth it out.

A nervous gesture, perhaps? Kate wondered. When she saw how it pressed tightly against Allegra's figure, and how the captain's eyes lingered a second too long before looking away, Kate thought it might have been a careful maneuver.

"I'm sorry," the captain said sadly, the barest hint of a blush in his cheeks. "I hate to say this, but if you're right about him using his guns on you, we'd have been able to arrest him if we'd arrived just a bit later."

"Only that might have been too late for us," Kate muttered. "Or at least one of us."

The captain nodded in agreement. "Look, kids, frankly, I believe your story. But Chernak's boat is clean. His men have licenses for those weapons. It's security for his import/export business, if you care to believe that. Even the drugs are gone. You had them, but you don't anymore."

"But if we'd kept them, you'd never have believed us," Justin pointed out.

"That may be true," the captain admitted. "It's moot now, though. We have no evidence, and in our country, well-founded suspicion isn't enough to take someone to court. Most of the time, that's the right thing. In this instance, it's unfortunate. We know what Chernak does, but he's awfully careful. He always has been. He claims he was sending his men to shore to rescue you."

"That's a laugh," Allegra choked out. "He doesn't 'rescue' people who run away from him."

"Listen, you'll stay on board tonight," the captain announced. "I'm sending two small boats to escort Chernak back home. You'll be safe here, okay? And tomorrow I'll give you a chance to get the rest of your stuff, and anything you want to salvage from your boat. And then we'll take you home."

"Home?" Kate and Justin said together.

"Well," the captain chuckled. "I spent a few summers of my own in Ocean City. Much as I'd love to go back, I'm afraid we can't take you that far. Home to the States, anyway. We'll help you out. Don't worry."

That was a laugh, Kate thought. Don't worry? When you've thrown away the stash of a notorious drug smuggler, and he's still free to do something about it? She sighed as Justin pulled her into his arms. No, Chernak wouldn't follow them all the way to O.C. It was a business decision. He just lost out this time. No way would he travel that far for nothing.

Nothing but revenge, she couldn't help but think.

EIGHT

"You asleep?" Justin whispered down to her.

Kate shook her head, and then realized he couldn't see her in the darkness. "No." She sighed quietly. "A little wound up, I guess."

She heard the sound of Justin shifting in his bunk, and the soft creak of springs. A soft thud next to her, and then she felt his weight on her mattress.

"Don't mind me," he whispered. "I just can't lie there and talk to the ceiling. You okay?"

"Mmm." She nodded. She went to sit up and misjudged the space under Justin's bunk, hitting her head against the bed frame. "Ouch!" She was trying to be quiet, and so she bit on her finger until the throbbing went away.

"Kate?"

"I'm just trying to make some space for

you," she muttered, pushing back against the wall. "Luxury accommodations these aren't. Even the *Kate* had more room."

She heard his soft sigh.

"Oh, Justin, I'm sorry."

"It's okay," he said as he lowered himself down beside her. "I'm just glad we're safe." They lay still for a moment, cramped into the tiny bunk, listening to Allegra's slow, rhythmic breathing from the other side of the small room.

"Are you sure she's asleep?" Kate asked, her voice tight.

"Yeah. Kate?" Justin paused, and Kate could almost hear him searching for words. "I was scared today, on the beach."

She reached out and grabbed his hand. He held her fingers tightly. "It was almost like the last time," he continued, "when I thought I was drowning, and all I could think of was you."

"I'm glad we were rescued," she said, her throat tight.

"I was afraid," Justin went on. "I was afraid that you would be hurt and I couldn't do anything for you."

"Justin, please." Kate sighed. "Let's not think about it." She shivered and shook her head. "I'm just glad it's over."

"Kate, I'm sorry for the last few days—"

"No, Justin. I'm sorry. Look, I still don't trust

Allegra at all. I can't trust her. Not even as far as I could throw her, and in my slightly crippled state," she wiggled the toe on her sprained foot, "that wouldn't be very far at all."

"I don't really trust her either, Kate," Justin admitted. "But while we were stuck there . . . I was just trying to keep the peace a little. I hope you understand that. I was never . . . against you, or anything like that."

"But peace isn't what Allegra wanted," Kate said before she could help herself. "She wanted you."

Justin squeezed her fingers. "Don't I get a say in any of this?" He laughed softly. "You're jealous, you know, Kate Quinn. Jealous like any woman in love."

"Well, shouldn't I be?" she asked in the darkness.

"You definitely should be in love," Justin whispered. He moved away then, and in a moment she felt his arms sliding under her.

"Justin?"

He pulled her carefully from the bunk and stood, holding her against his chest.

"And you definitely shouldn't be jealous," he continued. Her fingers clutched at his shoulders as he raised her onto his bed.

"Justin," Kate whispered, "what are you doing! We're not alone in here."

Justin pulled himself up onto the bunk after her, pushing her up against the wall. She felt the length of him stretch out beside her. He took her hand.

"First," he said, ticking off the reasons on her fingers, "she's asleep. Second, we'll be very quiet. And third"—Justin took that finger and brought it to his lips, kissing the tip of it—"I've missed you."

Kate sighed as her stomach dropped and disappeared. "I've missed you, too," she said just before his lips found hers.

The next morning the captain lent Justin a launch to use to retrieve the rest of their stuff. After he'd dropped Allegra and Kate back on the beach to collect what they'd already managed to salvage, he turned the boat toward the sorry wreck that had once been the *Kate*. Allegra watched him drop anchor, wondering how much he would actually bring up. She had to figure out what she was going to do with the cocaine she'd hidden. Maybe Justin would salvage enough so that she could smuggle it aboard again. . . .

"Kate, listen," Allegra said brightly. "I'm just going to go and have one last quick dip in the little pool, okay? Now that we're rescued, it's become a lot more beautiful. I'd like to enjoy it before I leave."

Kate was already busy filling one of the small duffels they'd been given to use.

Allegra fisted the small duffel bag she'd brought into a ball and held it behind her back, but Kate didn't even turn to look at her.

"Sure, Allegra," she replied icily. "You know where I'll be. Just don't take too long. Justin's probably almost done, and we'll be leaving right after that. I'm sure even you don't want to hold up the Coast Guard."

"Of course not, Kate," Allegra said sweetly as she started to back toward the trees. *You snot*, she thought. *You think you're so smart. And you wouldn't trust me as far as you could throw me? You have no idea what I'm capable of.*

When she hit the trees, she turned and ran along the beach until she was out of sight of the cove. She found the big tree that was her marker, walked ten steps out, dropped to her knees, and began to dig. In a few minutes she'd uncovered her stash.

Pathetic, really, compared to what had been there, she thought angrily. Goddamn that Chernak for following them! And damn the island for being in the way when she changed the boat's course to escape. And damn Justin for finding the cocaine.

Allegra felt sick when she remembered diving

down with him to get rid of it all. All that money puffing away into wet white clouds.

All that money that was *supposed* to take care of her for life! Was she supposed to have put up with Chernak all that time for nothing? He'd needed constant stroking, Allegra remembered, to keep his arrogance intact. He played the role of drug smuggler to the tee, with those ridiculous white suits and bikini-clad women lounging around the pool all day. Allegra recalled how often she'd had to choke back her laughter and play the simpering fool. Allegra had paid her dues if anybody had.

When she'd found out what he was doing with the abandoned boat, she knew it was the opportunity she'd been waiting for. And it should have been so easy! Catch a ride with a couple of do-gooder naive fools and steal the drugs from them before Chernak could retrieve them.

Anger burned through her. She'd have shot Justin and Kate herself if it could have saved the stash, but there'd have been Chernak to deal with anyway.

And the damn Coast Guard. She couldn't curse them enough, if the idiots couldn't find a way to put Chernak in jail. But now the Coast Guard, and its handsome, easily manipulated captain, was her salvation, though the thought almost made her laugh out loud.

Well, at least she had this, Allegra thought, looking at the four carefully wrapped bricks of cocaine she'd hidden. It was still worth a lot of money. At least enough to start that new life of hers.

All she had to do was *get it back home*. But how?

"You have the nerve," she told herself, "that's not even a question. The *question* is, how suspicious *are* Kate and Justin? If they get you caught, that's it. You won't be able to cry or tease your way out of it."

Allegra sat on the sand for another moment, weighing her options. Then she grabbed the bricks of cocaine and stuffed them into the small duffel. She had no choice now, no matter how risky it was. There was *no way* she wasn't going to get what she deserved after all this.

Justin looked out at the reefs they'd sailed through, and the one that had finally stopped them. The water, even at twenty and thirty feet, was crystal clear, clear enough for Justin to see exactly how badly damaged the *Kate* really was. Even if they'd managed to crash near a marina, or at least on an inhabited island, there would have been nothing he could have done to save his boat. It was totaled. He'd have been lucky to sell it for parts.

Justin stroked his way through the gaping hole in the *Kate*'s hull and into the tiny galley. He remembered all the hours he'd put into the boat back in Ocean City. He had kept it in the boat house where he lived, so that he was never more than thirty feet away from it. And when he'd put in the tiny cots and the small stove, when he'd filled the small cupboards he'd made by hand, the plan had never been to swim through it all later. It was like a nightmare. Only he knew he wasn't dreaming.

Justin shook his head, his hair floating back and forth in the water, and started grabbing what he could get while his breath of air lasted. His fingers opened a cabinet, and his old camping gear floated up in front of him. He reached out and pinched a few pots and pans from the water, tucked some of the canned goods into his shorts. He took anything he saw—even the tiny curtains he'd put in for Kate—however silly it seemed.

Because none of it was silly. It had all been his.

He swam away from the boat and started to drift back to the surface. He could see the sunlight falling into the water, playing off the surfaces of the boat, shimmering in strange patterns, a glint of metal on deck. Justin swam over and reached down. It was the brass nameplate he'd fixed to the compass housing.

He wrapped the booty in the curtains, shoved the bundles under his arm, and pulled a tiny screwdriver from the back pocket of his shorts. His fingers were getting sluggish. He was running out of air. He tried to work the screwdriver faster. He brushed away the tiny screws as they came loose, and they floated off soundlessly. Finally he pulled the nameplate free.

He fingered it gently, drawing each of the letters out as though it would help him remember. KATE. It had been the last piece of work he'd done to the boat. The last thing he'd done the day he left Ocean City.

Justin's lungs were about to burst. And with all the saltwater around him, he couldn't say whether or not he was crying.

"Kate?"

Kate turned at the sound of her name and found Allegra, back from her little good-bye trip to the waterfall.

"Yes?"

"I packed up my stuff," Allegra said, kicking one of the small duffel bags the Coast Guard had given them. "This one's mine. Okay?"

"Fine," Kate replied, turning away. *What's her problem? Does she think I'm going to try and steal all the seashells she collected? It's not like she has all her worldly possessions with her on the island.*

"I hope Justin finds my bag on the boat," Allegra said, looking out at the Kate.

Kate remembered that when they'd first left the Bahamas, she'd stowed Allegra's bag for her. It had spilled open, and Kate had found herself looking at what might have passed for a sample sale from the Victoria's Secret catalogue. She realized that that had been the first surprise from their new "naive and dorky" hitchhiker, or whatever the appropriate term was for someone you picked up on your sailboat.

"I'm all packed," Allegra continued, squinting out over the water to the Coast Guard ship bobbing on the waves.

"Yep." Kate followed her gaze, and then glanced back at her.

"So I doubt there's room for anything else."

"I hear you, Allegra," Kate finally said in exasperation. "I don't care about your stuff, all right? Should we find a marker so you can put your name on the bag? Is there anything else you need to tell me?"

Allegra gave her a long, hard stare.

"Well?" Kate pressed. "Aren't you going to find a way to toss that back in my face? Tell me that I must not know what it's like to only have enough possessions to fill one small duffel? Boo hoo. Does this mean that for once you don't have a reply? I'm astounded."

"Oh, no, Kate," Allegra replied coldly. "I'm the one who's astounded. I guess having your hurt ankle and all, and not being able to do much but pack a little bag, is really getting to you." She sighed casually and turned to watch Justin out at the remains of the Kate. "I'll just go help Justin finish up at the boat. And I'll let him know how testy you are. I'm sure *he* won't want to say the wrong thing and have you bite *his* head off."

Kate rolled her eyes as Allegra sauntered down to the water and dove in. Kate watched her stroke steadily out to the launch and pull herself into it. Allegra stood, her tanned body glistening, and wrung out her hair and stretched. Kate glanced at the Coast Guard cutter and noticed a few sailors on deck watching Allegra's little show.

"Ugh, she makes me sick," Kate muttered. This jealousy she couldn't quite shake was really eating at her. Kate had never thought of herself as that kind of person, but it was true—whenever Allegra was around, Kate did turn into a bit of a shrew. She just hoped Justin wasn't noticing too much.

Justin pulled himself from the water then, too. Kate watched as he spoke to Allegra, gesturing below him a few times and then turning away. *Thank you, Justin, for not staring*, she thought silently.

Kate sat on the beach for the next twenty minutes and watched Allegra and Justin take turns diving from the small launch into the water next to the *Kate*'s broken hull.

Each time they broke the surface, they rose clutching something in their hands, mostly clothing it looked like, various pieces of brightly colored material that they tossed into the little boat.

"Well, what do you expect? There's nothing else to save anyway," Kate told herself quietly. She knew that the only thing that really mattered was the boat itself. There was no way to rescue all the hours—all the dreams of travel and adventure—that Justin had put into her.

What would he do when they got back to O.C.?

Finally it looked like they'd had enough. Allegra was about to dive again, but Justin motioned for her to sit down, and started the little launch engine before she could argue. He turned the boat toward shore, where Kate was sitting with their stuff.

Allegra leaped nimbly out of the little boat before Justin even hit the sand. Kate stood, hobbled over to the bags, and reached down to pick up two of the small duffels at her feet. Just as she got her hands around the straps, Allegra was beside her, snatching one of them from her fingers.

"What's wrong with you?" Kate snapped, looking startled.

"This one's mine," Allegra replied calmly, clutching the small bag tightly in her fingers. "I told you that already."

Kate shook her head and gave her a long look. *Something is going on with her,* Kate thought. *I know it. I just don't know what it is.*

"Anything wrong?" Justin asked, coming up behind them.

"Nothing at all," Kate replied through gritted teeth. *Except I'd like to string Allegra up by the neck and never see her again.*

"Well, say good-bye to our little place in the sun," Justin smiled.

"Careful," Kate warned, shooting an icy glance at Allegra. "Elizabeth Taylor dies in that movie."

"What movie?" Justin asked.

"*A Place in the Sun,*" Kate said.

"Don't be so morbid." Allegra sighed. She turned to Justin and smiled brightly. "It's actually quite beautiful here, now that we don't have to worry about being rescued. Don't you think?"

Justin shook his head and laughed stiffly. "Actually, Allegra, I can't say I'm in the mood to appreciate the natural beauty of this place at the moment. We did just finish scavenging my boat."

"I'm sorry," Allegra said, putting a hand out to touch his arm. "How insensitive of me."

How dare you, you mean, Kate thought, watching Allegra's hand linger a bit too long for her liking.

Justin stepped away, toward the launch.

"Let's get going. Do you need any help, Kate?"

She followed after him, hobbling only a little now. Her ankle was still stiff and sore, but its size and color were just about normal.

"Just a little help, maybe," Kate said, putting her arms on Justin's shoulders. He lifted her, pausing and holding her in midair so that their eyes were level. Then he kissed her quickly on the mouth. Before she could say anything, he'd put her into the launch and turned back for their bags.

Once they were all settled, Justin pushed the boat into the water and steered them toward the cutter. Kate noticed that Allegra was unusually silent, gripping the bag she held on her lap as though it were a life preserver.

"I brought this up for you," Justin said, pulling something from his pocket and tossing it to Kate.

She looked down at the little brass nameplate in her hands, and instantly a lump formed in her throat.

"Are you sure you want me to have it?" Kate asked, wiping her eyes quickly as she pretended to push her hair back from her face.

"It was always for you anyway," Justin said. "And I have a feeling that after all this, I'll never be able to convince you of how great life on the water can be."

"Well," Kate answered softly, as the launch pulled up beside the cutter and ropes were tossed down to them, "don't count yourself out yet. I might be persuaded to give you another chance."

Justin tossed their two bags up to the waiting crew members and lifted Kate up into their arms. Allegra stood uneasily behind him. Justin reached for her bag, but she shook her head.

"I'll just hold it," she said, stepping up beside him, "if you can give me a boost too."

Kate watched from the deck as the top of Allegra's head came into view.

"Give us the bag," one of the crew said, "and we can help you."

Just then Allegra reached out an arm, and more of her came into view than anyone expected.

"Oops!" she cried, mortified, as her bikini top untied around her neck and slipped down. She tried to pull it back into place, but she wouldn't let go of her bag. The crew seemed particularly stunned, and Kate wondered how long it had been since the last time they'd gotten to shore. Finally the biggest of them, well over six feet and burly as an ox, reached out and plucked Allegra, bag and all, from Justin's grasp.

"Can you take me to our room?" Allegra cried, turning her bright red face into his shoulder.

"Sure I can," he said, happily hustling her away.

Why is it that she never misses an opportunity for an entrance? Kate wondered, shaking her head.

NINE

Chelsea opened her eyes to the soft hum of a motorboat passing the beach out back. A hot bolt of sunlight cut across her like a beauty queen's sash. She sat up, disoriented to find herself sprawled out on the couch. For a second, she didn't know why she was here in Grace's living room.

Why wasn't she across the street, in bed with Connor?

For that second, her life was in one piece instead of shattered like a bathroom mirror; for that second, she hadn't seen Antonio in years and she and Connor were fine, a little testy, but still fine; for that second, she'd never gone down to the christening in Washington, and Connor was plowing through his book, moving slowly toward the stardom that awaited him at the end of the dark tunnel he was in.

But she had gone to the christening, and she had seen Antonio, and her marriage to Connor was not fine but in serious jeopardy. She rose slowly, her muscles stiff and sore. She stood and walked over to the glass doors that led out to the deck.

If I'm going to be staying here now, I really ought to sleep in a bed, she thought. *Particularly since I even have my old room back.*

She squinted through the window and couldn't understand how she could be so miserable on a beautiful day like this.

"Where is everybody?" she asked, looking around the room. She couldn't hear a thing. Well, there were three possibilities: Either everyone was still asleep, or they hadn't even come home last night, or they already had great plans for the day and they were gone. They probably were all out having the time of their lives. Who would want to baby-sit her?

Chelsea dragged herself to the upstairs bathroom and looked at herself in the mirror. She looked like she'd walked all night through a storm.

"That's the good thing about living in a beach town," she said to herself. "Everyone has that drowsy, windblown look."

She rubbed her fingers across her teeth, went back to her room, and threw on a bikini and a pair of shorts. She quickly called the office to let them know she wasn't feeling well and wouldn't be in. Then she headed for the front door, but stopped before she opened it. The last thing she needed to see this morning was the house across the street that she used to live in.

Her old apartment. How sad. Well, it was still Connor's apartment. And that was even more sad. If she walked outside now, she might catch Connor's new writing "tutor" tripping out the front door, buttoning up her shirt, heading groggily for her sleek red sports car with that oh-so-satisfied leer plastered across her face. She could picture Connor on their balcony, with a skimpy towel wrapped around his little waist, waving at her retreating car, yelling, "I'll see you at your place for dinner!"

At the thought of that, Chelsea turned around and left the house through the back door leading to the beach.

The sunlight was blinding, and for a second—just for a second—Chelsea felt cheered. She hadn't even realized she was giving herself a day off from work until this second, and the thought made her happy, like giving herself a little gift.

Out on the water, the colorful triangles of windsurfers crisscrossed every which way. The bigger, elegant white billows of sailboats trailed along the horizon, moving slowly from nowhere to nowhere. The sand was dotted with sunbathers. Up and down the beach, she could see Grace's beach stands already open for business.

"Another day, another O.C. dollar," Chelsea said aloud.

Where was she going? She had no idea. She decided to just walk and go where her feet took her. Her life seemed directionless at the moment anyway. Why not take advantage of it and have a little adventure?

She quickly found herself on the boardwalk. The wood planks were warm and surprisingly soft under her bare feet. Most of the shops weren't open yet, but every few feet she caught the smell of bacon grease and fried eggs on the stiff breeze, wafting over from the Beachfront Diner. The sea gulls stood in packs, looking this way and that, as if they didn't know where to go.

"Too early for them, too," Chelsea guessed.

She stretched her arms up toward the sun. Something about the day was so freeing—she almost felt that if she started flapping her arms, she'd fly.

She knew what it was. She was all cried out. Last night she'd sobbed herself to sleep. There wasn't a tear, or an ounce of sadness, left in her.

She walked and walked toward the outskirts of town. Then she stopped dead in her tracks.

She couldn't believe it. Was this why she had gone for a walk? She couldn't believe that part of her could be so devious, and the rest of her so innocent.

She found herself standing in front of the Watercrest Motel. A long, one-story, shabby-looking place with turquoise shutters and pink doors and a sandy parking lot. Just like a hundred other motels in Ocean City. Except that somewhere inside this one slept Antonio Palmer, Midshipman, U.S. Navy.

When he'd told her yesterday where he was staying, she hadn't thought she was registering the name in her brain. She definitely didn't know where it was. So how did she end up here? It was like someone was guiding her, pushing her out the back door, along the boardwalk, past the center of town, where she'd never been in her life. As if she'd been led here by a higher power.

Chelsea shook her head. Looking at the motel, she knew exactly what that higher power was—it was called good old-fashioned desire.

One door at the very end was flung open. It was like a sign. Chelsea smiled and walked across the parking lot. Sure enough, the rented car parked in front had D.C. plates. And as she stepped into the doorway, not an ounce of her was surprised to find Antonio with his feet on the bed and his hands pressed on the floor, his head bobbing up and down as he did a set of push-ups. Chelsea smiled: just like a good naval middie.

What did surprise her was not what he was doing, but what he looked like: his body was board straight, his back parted down the middle by two firm ridges of rock-hard muscle. His shoulders were like bags of stone, and his arms were like pistons made of steel. There wasn't a smidgen of fat anywhere. Better yet, he was covered in a layer of sweat that made him look varnished, like a painted statue.

Even the way he grunted the number of repetitions with each push-up—". . . forty-six, forty-seven . . ."—made Chelsea smile. If she denied her attraction to him, she knew she'd be lying. Besides, what would be the purpose? It was a beautiful, sunny day, and she felt free as a bird. . . .

"Fifty," Antonio groaned, then lowered his feet off the bed and sat like a stone Buddha. It took him a few seconds to realize that Chelsea was standing in the doorway, and when he did, an expression half of horror and half of pleasure crossed his face.

"Ch-chels—" he stammered.

Chelsea flashed him a gleaming smile, and all he could do was grin in return.

"I'm glad you decided to come," he said. "I didn't think you'd heard the address."

"I didn't think I had either," Chelsea said. Her eyes wandered around the shabby motel room. An awful painting of a ship in stormy seas hung at a slant above the bed. "Nice room, sailor," she said.

Antonio stood to his full height of six foot two and smiled shyly. "So long as it keeps me near you," he said quietly.

Chelsea didn't hide her admiration for Antonio's sleek, conditioned body, and Antonio obviously didn't seem to mind either.

"Let me get some clothes on," he said slowly, reaching for a T-shirt on the bed.

Chelsea laughed. "Don't do it on my account."

Antonio took a step toward her. He was giving off heat like a furnace.

"Why the sudden turnaround?" Antonio asked. "I was beginning to believe I didn't have a chance with you, Chels."

"I left Connor," she said.

Antonio looked concerned. "Are you okay?" he asked.

"I am now," Chelsea said, glancing at his washboard abdomen.

"Really?" Antonio's face was full of childlike hope, like a boy hearing that he was going to his first baseball game.

"Really," Chelsea said. "So, have you had breakfast?"

Antonio looked at her meaningfully. "Not yet," he said.

"How about the diner?" Chelsea said, even as Antonio was walking toward her.

His arms swept under hers. "I think I have everything I could want right here," he said.

She could smell his musky sweat as he bent down. She lifted her face, and the kiss was like going home, soft and strong, safe and dangerous all at the same time. After all, she was still a married woman. She pressed her body against his. He drew her toward the bed . . .

But she stopped in her tracks, breathing hard, and when she opened her eyes, despite everything that had happened, she was surprised to find Antonio standing before her. It wasn't as though she'd expected Connor—Connor, for one thing, could never even dream about having Antonio's biceps—but she felt like she might be moving too quickly. After all, out on that boardwalk, she sort of liked that newfound feeling of freedom. Even if she and Connor were done, did she really want to jump right into a relationship with Antonio, as inviting as he was?

Antonio sat on the bed and took Chelsea's hands. She stood before him. He pressed the side of his face to her belly.

"Maybe . . ." Antonio began, then stopped. "Oh, forget it."

"What?" Chelsea prodded him. She lifted his face in her hands. He was so handsome. Still, there was some thin wall between them, something keeping her from leaping into his arms.

"I don't know," he said. "I was just thinking . . ."

"Don't strain yourself, Antonio," Chelsea laughed. "There's smoke coming out of your ears."

Antonio put his ear to Chelsea's chest.

"I can hear your heart beating," he said.

She kissed the top of his head.

"I was just thinking . . ." he began again.

"You were just thinking," Chelsea prompted him.

"That wouldn't it be nice if one day we had a baby," he blurted.

Chelsea lifted his chin and peered into his eyes. "Are you serious, Antonio?"

"I've known you almost my whole life," he said. "It's not like I wouldn't know what I was getting into. I love your family. And I think they'd feel all right about me—"

"They love you, Antonio," Chelsea said. "B.D. would love it if you were his brother-in- . . ."

She couldn't finish. Brother-in-law? What were they talking about!

"Have you and Connor gotten lawyers yet?" Antonio asked.

"Lawyers!"

"You know, to clear up any legal snags about splitting up."

Chelsea laughed ruefully. "First of all, we don't have anything to split up, except Connor's typewriter, and I wouldn't want that anyway. But second of all, I don't know about divorce—"

"But you left him, right? I mean, you just said you left him."

"I left him, yes," Chelsea said. "But I don't know if I've *left* him left him." She released herself from his powerful hands and paced back and forth across the room. "I mean, Antonio, divorce? Do you know what that would do to my parents?"

"You think they'd rather you be miserable for the rest of your life, trapped in a terrible marriage?"

Miserable? Trapped? Terrible marriage? It was okay for her to be critical of Connor and their marriage, but she didn't like to hear anyone else cut him, or it, down like that.

Chelsea held up her hands, as if demanding that Antonio stop where he was, even though he wasn't moving.

"Whoa, boy," she said. "I don't know. Maybe

we're getting ahead of ourselves here. I mean, you still have your naval career—"

Antonio reached out and snatched Chelsea by the hands and tugged her close. She stood between his legs. He wrapped his arms around the back of her legs.

"I'd drop the Navy in a second if it meant it would give you and me a chance," he said.

Chelsea stopped breathing. Up until this very moment, all this was almost a fairy tale. She and Connor were having their problems and seemed on the verge of splitting up, but nothing was permanent. She hadn't done anything yet that couldn't be undone. If Antonio gave up his commission in the Navy, he wouldn't be able to go back. Is that what she wanted?

"You mean you'd give up your career, everything you've worked for your whole life, to be with me?"

Antonio stood and took her in his powerful arms. "I'd give up my world any day as long as I could live in yours," he said.

"Would the Navy even let you go?"

Antonio put his finger to his lips. "There are always ways out," he said.

"But your mother—you promised your mother . . ."

"She'd understand."

Chelsea doubted that. Mrs. Palmer was a career officer in the Marines who had devoted her entire life to the military. She'd been killed during the Gulf War, and Chelsea knew that it was because of her that Antonio had entered the naval academy. Would he break a promise to his dead mother just for Chelsea?

"But divorce," Chelsea whispered, as though to herself.

She felt her face being lifted, and as Antonio's closed in, his mouth nearing hers, she peered at him wide-eyed: handsome, even beautiful, strong yet gentle, intelligent, ambitious. And black, she thought. It would be easier; there were certain advantages. Life as one half of a "mixed marriage" hadn't exactly been a piece of cake. . . .

Her mind argued a pretty strong case for Antonio, but her heart seemed to be crying, Wait a second!

Advantages? Easier? What was this about, anyway? Was this about love, or about applying for a job?

Chelsea responded to Antonio's throbbing kiss with one of her own. Her fingers played over his back, and she couldn't help fantasizing what would happen if she gave him just a little shove into the bed behind him. But she pulled her lips away and lay her head against his chest, as though ducking away from the wind. She heard his heart beating, steady and loud.

Just like him, she thought: dependable, consistent.

A picture of Antonio flashed through her brain: of she and Antonio surrounded by their children, and he was stern, almost sour, a strict disciplinarian, not letting the kids just cut loose. Not how Connor would have been, taking their boys or girls by their hands and flipping them all over the house until they were bursting with giggles and their faces were split in agonizing laughter. Connor the lovable clown, Antonio the . . . the what? Their future was like a picture frame without the picture.

And there it was—she couldn't deny it. It wormed its way through her heart and was poking at her: the sinking feeling that this train was not only traveling just a bit too fast, but maybe going down the wrong set of tracks.

TEN

What a day, Grace thought as she made her morning rounds. The sun was bright, and there was a good breeze up on the water. She noticed some well-tanned men running out into the surf with their boards tucked under their arms.

Business was brisk at most of her stands. Grace asked all her employees about the previous day's tally and shared some good customer gossip. She stopped and chatted with Roan for a few minutes, and Bo, of course, who shadowed Roan at work, no doubt to make sure that other guys couldn't hit on her. Grace found herself getting into a better mood as she worked her way down the beach.

But it wasn't because she was approaching Carr's lifeguard stand. It was Wilton she was looking forward to seeing.

"Hey there." Grace leaned around the corner of Wilton's stand and found him, as she expected, with his nose buried in another book. She went closer and peeked over his shoulder. James Joyce, *Ulysses*.

"You'd better be careful," Grace continued. "At the rate you're going, you'll have read all the Great Books there are by the end of the summer. And then what will you do when you get back to school?"

Wilton carefully turned down the corner of the page and closed the book. Then he looked up at her and nodded.

"Hello, Grace," he said, brushing his brown hair from his eyes. He was squinting up at her, his hazel eyes catching the sunlight and looking almost golden. Pale freckles spotted the bridge of his nose and his cheeks. Grace found herself looking at his mouth, a straight serious line. For a moment his solemn gaze looked almost predatory, and Grace shivered.

Then she burst out laughing. "I don't know why it is," she admitted, "but your characteristically enthusiastic greetings get me right where it counts." She patted her hand over her heart.

Wilton's eyes followed her hand, and when he realized what he was looking at, he cleared his throat and turned away. Grace could see a slight blush in his cheeks, and somehow his reaction made her feel very sexy.

"By the way, I figured you wouldn't do that," she said.

"Do what?" Wilton replied strangely, still looking away from her.

Grace smiled. *Look at my chest*, is what she wanted to say, just to see his reaction.

"Crease the corners like that," Grace replied instead, gesturing to the big book on his lap. "I figured being such a book lover, you'd have a collection of bookmarks to use. But you ruin the pages just like me."

"No." Wilton shook his head. "I don't ruin the pages. It's the ideas in the book that you need to treasure and respect. Of course you should respect the book, too, and that means not ripping out the pages, I guess. But a book is just an object, after all."

Wilton looked down at the old volume in his lap and gently ran his fingers across the cover. Grace noticed his fingers were long and delicate. She found herself wondering if his touch would be that gentle on a living body.

"It's meant to be held and read and used," Wilton continued. "And if you're afraid of creasing it or marking it up a little, you can't really enjoy it." Wilton paused and pursed his lips. "That's how I feel, anyway," he concluded.

Grace nodded, dumbfounded. "Well," she responded, "no one could ever accuse you of not feeling strongly about things, could they?"

"Of course not," he answered matter-of-factly. "Everyone feels strongly about things. I know you do. It's just that sometimes people are afraid to admit to how they feel." He turned to look at her. "In case someone else disagrees. Feelings make you vulnerable."

Grace nodded, and sank down into the sand next to Wilton's chair. She thought of David, suddenly, about telling him how important freedom was to her. About how she wanted to travel. When David had told Grace he was leaving, she was hurt, but she couldn't argue. They both knew how she felt.

"And people remember what you say," Grace sighed. "You can't keep changing your feelings about something just to protect yourself."

"That's exactly right," Wilton agreed. "It sounds like you know human nature pretty well."

Grace smiled, strangely pleased at the compliment. "Well, it's not human nature in general as much as my own," she admitted.

"Then that's even better," Wilton replied. "Most people don't know their own natures, let alone anyone else's. Speaking of feelings, I was sorry you couldn't join me last night," Wilton said, reaching out to briefly touch Grace on the shoulder. "They showed some of the best old *F-Troop* episodes. I think you would have enjoyed it."

"I probably would have," Grace admitted, sifting sand through her fingers. Wilton's touch *was* gentle, and Grace was surprised at how nice it had felt.

She thought of how she'd blown Wilton off the night before, and she wondered whether or not she should tell him what she'd done instead. Considering what they were talking about, and the fact that Ocean City was a very *small* town, she figured she should. She just had to extricate herself from her little white lie.

"I actually didn't get to go over to Marta's last night," Grace said. "She called to cancel just after I spoke to you."

"You should have come over then," Wilton replied. "Better than staying home alone."

"Well, actually, I didn't stay home alone," Grace admitted. "Carr happened to be there when she called, and so he and I went out together."

"Oh," Wilton said flatly.

"What's that supposed to mean?" Grace asked, hearing the distinct sound of disapproval in the one word.

"It doesn't mean anything," Wilton said.

"Just 'Oh.' He's the one who lives with you? The lifeguard that all the girls on the beach are in love with, right?"

"That's him," Grace answered, for some reason embarrassed by Wilton's description. "But I'm not just one of the girls in love with him, you know."

"Why shouldn't you be?" Wilton answered, shrugging and sinking back into his chair. "You probably look great together."

"Don't say it like that," Grace snapped, standing up and brushing sand from her bottom. "That's not the reason I went out with him. And besides, it's not like we're going steady or anything. I *can* see other people."

"But why would you want to?" Wilton asked, opening his book again. "I'm sure he's everything a woman like you could ask for."

"How dare you say that to me," Grace cried, suddenly feeling like hitting him. "What do you mean by 'a woman like me'? You don't even really know me!"

"No," Wilton replied sadly, looking into her eyes, "I guess I don't."

Grace turned and stalked away quickly, unhappy and not sure why. Well, not wanting to admit why, anyway.

Wilton just wasn't interested in her. He obviously thought she was a bimbo or something, only interested in someone's looks. So what was the big deal about that? He was just a bookworm. Who even cared what he thought?

Grace snorted at herself, because she knew the answer. For some reason, she cared, and she really didn't know why.

ELEVEN

Late that afternoon, Grace and Chelsea found themselves wrestling with the blender.

"Whatever you do, don't forget the tiny little umbrellas," Marta called from the living room. "That's the only reason I agreed to come over here anyway."

Grace held the pulse button even while the motor began to grind, trying to turn two trays of ice cubes into a smooth slush.

"Careful," Chelsea warned, casually stepping away. "I smell smoke. Are you sure that thing isn't going to melt down?"

"I sure hope not," Grace replied, pouring a small pitcher of freshly squeezed lemon juice into the whining machine.

"Are you killing that thing?" Marta called out. "Should I call a mechanic?"

Chelsea shook four brightly colored drink umbrellas from the package and popped them open. Grace poured the frozen lemonade into four margarita glasses, and Chelsea stuck an umbrella in each one. They brought the tray into the living room, where Marta was sitting in her wheelchair.

Grinning broadly, Grace poked Chelsea in the ribs and pointed to Roan, who was lingering out on the deck, trying not to be obvious about wanting to hang out with them.

"Roan," Marta called sweetly, "don't you want to come in here and have a drink with us? Your guardian approves, since it *is* alcohol free. Unless of course you have something else to do, like watch the news or play solitaire?"

Roan poked her head into the living room. "Me?" she asked innocently. "You guys made one for me? Well, I'm supposed to call a friend, but—"

"Just say the word if you want to bag out on us old ladies," Grace chuckled. "We know you probably have better things to do."

"No, no." Roan came in quickly, going straight for the lone glass on the table and plopping herself down onto the floor. "Nothing better to do . . . at the moment."

"Ooh," Marta whispered. "Grace us with your presence."

"That's me, dear," Grace replied. "The one and only."

"Okay," Marta said, waving her glass, "now that I'm set up with a drink that won't do more than quench my thirst, it's on to the nitty-gritty details. You finally went out with Mr. Incredible? Don't keep us in suspense, please." Marta patted the purse that hung from her armrest. "I may be able to make more money from this deal. Another ten dollars says you kissed him."

"Don't make that bet," Chelsea warned.

"That's right." Grace laughed. "You'd better listen to Chelsea. She's the reason Carr and I didn't have the Big Kiss last night."

"What do you mean?" Marta asked.

"We were about one eyelash away from contact when Chelsea came barging through the door."

"Ohhh." Marta cringed. "That's awful. What about the other guy? Mr. Learned and Literal?"

"Does she mean Wilton?" Roan asked incredulously, slurping frozen lemonade from the side of her glass. "Are you interested in Wilton?"

"Get your eyes back in your head before I belt you," Grace snapped. "The answer to that question is none of your business. But just out of curiosity, what's wrong with Wilton, anyway?"

"Compared to Carr?" Roan asked, as though there was no comparison. "Carr is gorgeous, and Wilton's . . . just Wilton. Carr has an awesome body, and Wilton has . . . a body. Carr's practically a god—I mean, he is just so *handsome*. And Wilton . . . Wilton's just a guy, you know? Like anybody."

"Wilton is definitely *not* 'like anybody,'" Grace and Marta replied at the same time.

"Well, there's no contest, in my book." Roan shook her head in amazement. "I can't even believe you can compare them."

"I guess that means you'd dump Bo if someone better-looking came along?" Marta asked, cocking her head and raising her eyebrow.

"Yeah," Grace said. "I'm interested in your answer to that, if you don't mind."

"What?" Roan asked, fidgeting. "I didn't say anything about dumping Bo."

"But you said there's no contest when it comes to looks," Marta pointed out.

"And that means that if someone like Carr asked you out, you'd have no problem getting rid of Bo," Grace finished.

"I would too have a problem," Roan replied. "I mean, only if I was going to dump him. I mean, that doesn't mean that I'd dump him—"

"But you might?" Marta asked.

"No!" Roan cried. "I mean, of course not. I wouldn't dump Bo. I love him."

"Well, I guess that means that some things

are more important than looks," Grace said. "Right, Roan?"

"Yeah, I guess." Roan nodded, scratching a mosquito bite on her arm. "So does that mean you're sorry you went out with Carr?"

Grace laughed. "Wait a minute, did I say that?"

"It sounds like you might have," Chelsea said.

"Well, don't let me misspeak myself," Grace drawled. "I most certainly am not sorry. And the only thing I am sorry about is that I didn't get a chance to kiss him."

"And I apologize—for the *eight hundredth* time," Chelsea added. "I promise I'll never interrupt you again."

"Well, don't worry, because I'm going out with him tonight." Grace sighed dreamily. "And we're going to go somewhere far, far away from you. You won't have the chance to interrupt us. You going out?" she asked Marta.

"Nah," Marta answered. "It's stay-at-home night tonight."

"So domestic," Grace sneered.

"Domestic bliss," Marta agreed.

Grace saw Chelsea cringe.

"We're going out too," Roan said, upending her glass and finishing it off.

"Well, you've got a curfew, young lady," Grace declared. "Just remember it."

"Oh, right," Roan said, shaking her head.

"Sure, hang out, fine, everything's cool, and then, *bam*—drop some kind of uncool parental thing on me."

"She ambushed you," Marta agreed.

"Hey, have a great time. Just stay away from Carr." Grace laughed. "We wouldn't want you to find yourself in an awkward position, confronted with all that *handsome*."

"That's right," Marta teased. "Steal her boyfriend and dump her brother—she'd kill you."

"I said I wasn't going to dump Bo!" Roan moaned.

"What! Dump me?" Suddenly Bo appeared in the kitchen doorway, his skateboard dangling from his hand, his jaw dangling at his chest. "Oh man, that is *cold*. What did I do to get that?"

"Oh, no!" Roan cried, looking around at them. "I'm not dumping you. Don't listen to them, Bo—they're just giving me a hard time."

Bo rolled his eyes, cringing in pain. "You guys are talking about me? Oh, man, I hate that. Why do you girls have to do that all the time? Always talking about guys, about dumping guys."

"Don't you want to know what she said?" Marta teased.

"She said something about me? Roan? To my own sister?"

"Shut up! I'm not dumping him!" Roan cried, jumping up and glaring at Marta.

Marta and Grace cracked up.

"You see," Roan said, relieved, going to Bo and draping her arm around him. "I didn't say anything. They're just teasing." She gave him a kiss on the cheek.

"Really?" Bo said, brightening visibly.

"Yeah," Roan replied, turning him around and steering him out of the room. "You know how they are. They just like to give guys a hard time."

"Yeah, I know," he replied. The sound of his door closing drifted back to the living room. Grace and Marta burst out laughing again.

"She knows me well," Grace sighed, twirling her tiny umbrella over her head. "And tonight, if all goes well, Carr's the one who'll be having a hard time."

"That's a bit of an obvious one, even for you, Grace," Marta snorted.

"Well, I'm a little out of practice," Grace admitted.

"Oh, really? I wonder how out of practice that might be." Marta fingered her handbag again. "Are you trying to tell me you don't think you'll be getting that kiss you keep talking about?"

"I have no idea where you're going," Chelsea pointed out. "You'll be all on your own."

"I plan on it," Grace said, smiling slyly.

* * *

"I told you that we were going *far away*," Grace teased as she walked with Carr into the sand dunes of the state park that evening. They were well north of the city. Behind them, down the long stretch of beach, they could see the distant lights of condos and upscale dance clubs.

"No hanging out at the amusement park tonight," she said. "Though I'm quite sure you could have won me many toys." She squeezed his biceps.

"This is nice." Carr sighed. "It's much quieter up here. It's the first time I've felt at all like I was at home."

"But no haystacks," Grace pointed out.

"Well," Carr said, "of course not. Why would you want them?"

Grace sighed. "To roll in?"

Carr looked at her blankly.

"Okay," she bravely tried again, "how about, 'No hay to have a toss in'?"

"Oh," Carr nodded, suddenly understanding. "You're right," he choked out. "No haystacks."

"Lucky for you, the sand is softer."

Grace stopped short, and they stood facing each other, standing in a small valley between two sand dunes. The evening breeze rustled the beach grass at their feet. Less than a hundred yards away was the relentlessly pounding surf.

"Carr?" Grace asked, stepping toward him.

"Remember where we were last night at around this time?"

He nodded, and she placed his hands on her hips.

"Well," Grace said softly, "confidentially, I've brought us as far away from Chelsea as possible. I'm sure we won't have the same trouble tonight."

"No, I don't see that we will," Carr agreed, bending down toward her.

"Oops, sorry, excuse me," a voice interrupted as Grace was pelted with sand. It hit the back of her head and her neck and slid right down into her dress.

"What!" she cried as she pulled away from Carr and began fiercely shaking her clothes. "What is this? A universal conspiracy?"

Grace turned to see a figure balancing precariously on top of the dune right behind them.

"I can't believe this," she muttered. "Wilton? Is that you?"

"Grace?" The figure took a step forward and then tumbled down the sand dune, spraying them again and landing in a heap at their feet. A long metal tube rolled to a stop in front of Grace.

"Is this yours, Wilton?" she asked incredulously. "Are you spying? Were you spying on us? On me?"

Wilton picked himself up from the ground and brushed off his pants. He rescued a notebook and a large ledger from the ground and shook them out. Then he stepped toward her and held out his hand.

"May I have that back?" he asked coolly.

"Are you going to answer me?" Grace sputtered, embarrassed and angry. "I never would have expected this from *you* of all—"

"It's a telescope, Grace," Wilton said calmly. "And it only focuses on things that are at least a few hundred thousand miles away."

"Oh," she said, chastened, feeling her face grow warm. "A telescope?"

"Small but powerful," Wilton acknowledged.

"So you're out here looking at the moon and stuff?" Carr asked skeptically.

"You can look at the moon without a telescope, of course," Wilton answered. "But for the rest of the 'stuff,' you need something stronger than the naked eye."

"Wilton, what are you doing out here?" Grace asked, handing the telescope back to him.

"Actually, earlier tonight I was reading translations from Galileo's notebooks. He talks a lot about the stars, about their movements and particular constellations. It gives you an idea of how he became convinced that Earth was not the center of the universe."

"A tragedy, I'm sure," Grace remarked.

"The authorities found his ideas blasphemous," Wilton continued, staring oddly at Grace. "And rightly so. He was, of course, suggesting something quite unbelievable—something that went against what had been *taught* was correct."

"Did we come out here for a lesson?" Carr muttered.

"For example," Wilton continued, "if I said that you weren't meant to date each other, and told you to go home now and not spend any more time together, no doubt I would be ridiculed."

"Ridiculed, and maybe something else," Carr agreed, narrowing his eyes. "Are you suggesting that?"

"Of course not," Wilton answered, still not taking his eyes off Grace. "I wouldn't presume to impose like that. The comment was made merely for the sake of argument, to make a point."

"I'm not quite sure *I* get the point," Grace said carefully.

"You're smart, Grace," Wilton said casually. "You will if you think about it."

"Listen, Will," Carr began, "it was nice running into you, but—"

"It's Wil*ton*. Not Will," Wilton replied stiffly.

"Right." Carr nodded. "Fine. But can't you find another place to do this?"

"Can't you?" Wilton shot back.

"I'll answer that the gentlemanly way," Carr said. "We'll leave you to your stars, and your . . . blaspheming."

Carr took Grace by the arm and turned her away from the sand dunes and back toward town. She craned her head back and saw Wilton watching her, his face blank, the telescope tucked under his arm. She raised her hand. She wanted to say *something*. She didn't know why she should, but somehow she felt guilty for her accusations, and for being caught with Carr.

Hey, she reminded herself suddenly, *he's the one who insulted you the last time you spoke. Get over it, Grace. He thinks you're a bimbo. And if he can't see the truth, he's not as smart as he thinks he is.*

TWELVE

"So," Bo said, "what's for dinner?" His entire upper half was inside the refrigerator as he picked his way through the shelves front to back. "Doesn't look like anyone's done any shopping lately," he added meaningfully.

Chelsea just laughed. "Uh-huh. I hate to break it to you, but I'm a terrible cook. And I don't do shopping."

"Really?" Bo pulled his head out of the dairy shelf and looked at Chelsea with surprise. "I thought all wives could cook—"

He couldn't stop himself in time.

"Sorry," he said, making a hasty retreat back into the fridge.

"No problem," Chelsea said. "Even though I'm here, I'm still somebody's wife. But that doesn't mean this wife can cook."

"That's okay," Bo said. "I'll just forage."

Before he could make a clean dive into the freezer, there was a knock at the front door. Bo and Chelsea looked at each other, but neither made a move.

"Will you get it, please?" Chelsea begged.

Bo screwed up his face in that especially annoying rebellious-teenager expression.

"Bo," Chelsea said threateningly, "I may be a guest in this house, but I am still your elder." She softened and began to plead with her eyes. "Please, Bo, please? Have a heart. If it's Antonio or Connor, just tell him I'm not here. Okay?"

"You mean you want me to lie?" Bo said with mock horror.

"Bo!" Chelsea snapped. "Come off it. My life may be at stake here."

"Ooh."

"If it's either one of them, I'll have a nervous breakdown. I need some breathing room. Some time to think."

"Uh-huh," Bo said, folding his arms, nodding profoundly.

The front door shook with somebody's pounding.

"Chelsea!" cried out a voice.

"Okay," Chelsea whispered, "it's Antonio. Just remember what I said. No matter what, no matter what he offers you, I'll double it. I'm—not—here."

"No sweat, Chels," Bo said nonchalantly, giving her the thumbs-up sign. "I lie all the time. This'll be a piece of cake."

Chelsea hid in the kitchen while Bo opened the door.

"Uh, hello," she heard Antonio say in his infinitely polite manner.

"May I help you?" Bo said with exaggerated politeness, and a slight bow.

"I'm looking for Chelsea Lennox," Antonio said, his voice suddenly louder.

Chelsea held her breath, realizing that Antonio had come into the house.

"Uh, hey there," Bo said. "Wait a second. Who are you, anyhow?"

"Antonio."

"Antonio," Bo said.

"Yeah," Antonio said, his voice pinched with annoyance. "Antonio. She'll know who I am."

"Well, she might or she might not," Bo said. "But we won't know for a while, because she isn't home right now."

"Isn't home?" Antonio said, his voice laced with surprise.

Chelsea frowned in the kitchen. *What, I should wait at home and be here for his every beck and call?* she thought.

"Well, it happens, you know?" Bo said. "Like, she went out. You know, as in: out of the house, into the world." He pointed out the door. "Out yonder."

Chelsea rolled her eyes. Come on Bo, she prayed. Don't overdo it—he's going to catch on.

She peered through the crack in the door, and sure enough, Antonio was looking suspiciously around the living room, as though Chelsea were camouflaged as a piece of furniture.

"So," Bo said. "Can I give her a message?"

"Yeah," Antonio said, still peering into the shadows underneath tables and chairs. "You can tell her I was here. Can you handle that?"

"Let me see," Bo said, squinting with concentration. "Let me see if I got that. You—were—here."

"And she better get the message," Antonio added, pointing his finger at Bo's chest. He stepped toward the door.

But just as Chelsea breathed a sigh of relief, she heard a familiar clearing of the throat. She peered through the door crack again.

Connor! she cried silently.

Connor was standing in the doorway, hands on hips, his face empty of expression. Dangling from the fingers of his right hand was a sheaf of papers. Chelsea squinted and recognized the blue-and-white logo of the phone company. He and Antonio were eyeing each other guardedly.

"Well, hello there Bo, my man," Connor said.

But he wasn't looking at Bo: He was looking straight at Antonio. "I've come to have a word with my wife."

"Uh, uh—" Bo stammered. He threw a panicked, SOS look back in Chelsea's direction.

"She's not home," Antonio said.

"And you are?" Connor said haughtily, as though to a servant.

In the kitchen Chelsea gritted her teeth. "You know damn well who he is," she said to herself. "And you probably saw him standing in the front door and rushed across the street, pretending you needed to talk to me about the phone bill."

"Antonio Palmer," Antonio said.

"Antonio Palmer, Antonio Palmer . . ." Connor said, squinting in the air, as though Antonio's identity were written across the ceiling.

"Look, man," Antonio said, "Let's stop the games. You know exactly who I am, and I know exactly who you are."

"Yes, yes, quite right," Connor chimed in his Irish lilt. "I seem to recall . . . you must be Chelsea's spin-the-bottle partner, the one from Granny's attic."

"Look, Connor, I'm not looking for trouble—" Antonio said.

"So you're just passing through Ocean City on your way up to . . . to . . . Where was that?"

"You know why I'm here in Ocean City," Antonio said grimly.

"For my wife," Connor said with a frown.

Antonio leveled a malevolent gaze at Connor. "Yes," he said proudly. "I am here for your wife. Except that she's not going to be your wife much longer."

Chelsea wanted to gag. What am I? she wondered. A piece of meat? A trophy? He's here for me, like he can just pick me up and cart me off like a package waiting for him?

"Oh, really?" Connor replied, surprised. "That's quite interesting news. Not my wife much longer?"

"That's right."

"And you've discussed this with her?"

"Yes, I have."

"And?" Connor said, challenging him.

"And, and . . ." Antonio was sputtering. "She's going to think about it."

"Oh, so now she's going to think about. I see. Yes, if I were you, I'd make that hotel reservation in Las Vegas right away, in time for your wedding at Ding Dong Chapel."

"Look, man," Antonio said, his face creased with rage. "What do you want with her?"

"What, am I suddenly persona non grata in the household of my good friends? Am I not permitted to cross the yellow lines in the street to come and have tea with my good friend Bo here, or with Grace? I didn't realize that since you rode into town on your white stallion my name is mud. But please, please, don't let me ruin your fantasy. Maybe if you concentrate really hard you can actually make me evaporate—poof!—before your eyes. Or better yet, blow a hole through my head with your Navy-issue pistol and pucker your lips and blow the smoke leaking from the barrel like Clint Eastwood. I understand how you American military types need to show off all that training, flex your muscles once a day, or else feel downright feminine."

Chelsea felt the grin at the corners of her mouth. Whatever she felt emotionally about Connor, there was no denying his wit, or his quick mind, or his Irish temper. Antonio just couldn't keep up.

"Look, Connor," Antonio said, waving his hand with frustration, "maybe you should just step away before this gets ugly. I didn't come here looking for trouble."

"Oh!" Connor exclaimed with mock surprise. "No, you didn't come looking for trouble. You just came looking for my wife!"

"What do you have there?" Antonio said, pointing at the paper in Connor's hand. "A phone bill? Is that Chelsea's phone bill? Is that why you're over here?"

"Yes, I see how perceptive you are, midshipman. Exactly. This is exactly my purpose in tiptoeing across the line in the sand outside. Chelsea's phone bill. I moonlight as a utilities collector."

Antonio tried to snatch the bill, but Connor pulled it away and held it over his head, as though from a child. "Now, now," Connor said.

"Look, I'll take care of it," Antonio said. "Give it to me, and I'll pay Chelsea's part of the bill."

Chelsea was doing all she could to keep herself from storming into the living room to break up this little meeting. She didn't like what she was hearing—from either of them: Connor's superior, cleverer-than-thou attitude, nor Antonio's assumption that everything had been decided and that she was his, his girl, his property. She didn't need anyone to pay her bills!

Suddenly it looked as if Antonio had decided to break Connor's neck. He stood toe to toe with him, his hands balled into fists. His mouth worked like he was trying to say something but couldn't get it out.

In the kitchen, Chelsea bit her knuckles.

Connor was just shaking his head, as if he was not in mortal danger. "You know, Antonio," he said, his eyes narrowed with his own totally cool brand of rage, "before you decide to break up a marriage by seducing someone else's wife, you should find out as much as you can about the object of your fascination. Because if you knew anything about Chelsea, you'd know that she'd never allow anyone to pay her bills, or talk about her the way you talk about her."

Chelsea felt herself nodding. She didn't want to feel like she was taking sides, but she couldn't help admitting that Connor knew her as well as she knew herself—maybe even better. He definitely knew her better than Antonio did. And for the first time, she realized that if she left Connor for Antonio, she'd have to start over completely. As beautiful as Antonio was, and as good friends as they once were, he was still, after all these years, a total stranger.

"Chelsea is as independent as anyone I've ever met," Connor was saying. "It's what I loved about her from the beginning, and I am not going to pass Chelsea on to you like a second-hand coat."

Connor pressed his finger against Antonio's chest as if he were the bigger and stronger of the two men, and Antonio, surprised, took a step backward.

"No matter what you think you know about her or yourself," Connor went on, "the fact is that you don't know what she needs. She is an artist. She'll always be an artist. You wouldn't understand that—"

"I can understand that—" Antonio said defensively.

"No, no you can't," Connor snapped, growing angry, jabbing at the air with his finger. "Anyone who pretends to the ideals of the U.S. Navy, but who commits the dishonor of spending his free time seducing another man's wife, would never, ever understand what I am trying to say. And don't you ever forget it, private."

"Midshipman," Antonio said, somewhat sadly.

"Whatever," Connor said, and, turning on his heels, stormed off the porch and across the street.

Antonio didn't move for a minute. He stood as if at attention, staring after Connor. Then, without looking at Bo, he strode out.

In the kitchen, Chelsea furiously rummaged through the drawers for a pen and paper. She found a pencil and an old grocery receipt. She quickly scrawled a message, *Meet me on the boardwalk in one hour*, folded it, and sprinted into the living room.

"Bo, go catch him and give him this!" she panted.

But Bo didn't move. He didn't even acknowledge her standing there. He was looking down at his shoes, in a state of shock.

"Bo," Chelsea said, shaking his arm.

Bo lifted his head. "Man, Chels, that was serious stuff. I haven't seen anything like that since the last Arnold Schwartzenegger movie. I thought Antonio was going to say, Hasta la vista, baby, and blow him away. Then I thought Connor was going to talk until Antonio got so confused his head would explode. Then I thought Antonio—"

"Bo!" Chelsea cried. "This isn't a movie. This is my life!"

"Well, it sure looks like a movie."

"Well, trust me, it's not. Here, take this," she said, stuffing the note into his hands, "and run and catch him and give it to him."

Bo took a step out, then stopped, turning around, looking very confused.

"Quick. Now. Right now!" Chelsea cried, giving Bo a shove out the door.

But Bo stopped and scratched his head. "Look Chelsea, I'm happy to help you if I can, but there's just one problem."

"What? What?" Chelsea asked impatiently.

"Which one do you want me to catch?" Bo asked.

THIRTEEN

"Are you sure you need to sleep?" Grace asked seductively, her arms wrapped loosely around Carr's neck. They were still out on the patio, leaning against the house in the shadows below the deck. Grace was making lazy patterns in the sand with her toe.

She'd finally gotten her kiss, and she had to admit, it was worth the wait. Carr was gorgeous and sexy, and there was definite chemistry between them.

"It's been a . . . really nice night, Grace," Carr said. It was dark, but she could still make out his blush. "I do need to sleep now, though. Lifeguarding, and all. I need to be well rested to do a good job."

"Yeah," Grace chuckled, "I've heard that one before."

"I bet your friend Justin didn't party too late, did he?" Carr said innocently.

"No, you're right," Grace acknowledged. "He didn't stay out all night, though sometimes he did stay *up* all night."

"What do you mean?" Carr asked. "He has insomnia?"

Grace sighed. *Kansas*, she reminded herself. *They must not have the same sense of humor out in Kansas.*

"How did he work if he didn't sleep?" Carr wondered.

"You do manage to bring him up at the strangest of times," Grace muttered.

"It's just that no one ever stops talking about him," Carr said sheepishly.

"You included," Grace pointed out.

"I'm just curious."

"Look, I love him," Grace said. "But he's not that mysterious. You'll meet him someday, I'm sure."

"Don't be mad, Grace," Carr said, stepping past her and sliding open the glass door. "Please don't be mad at me. I do need to get up in the morning."

He stood back to allow her access into the house, but she shook her head and stepped away.

"Well, *I* don't need to get up," Grace replied,

turning to the beach and the waves rolling into shore. "I'm going to take a little walk. Nighttime is my *favorite* time of day."

"Grace?"

Carr came up behind her and turned her slowly around. He leaned down and kissed her.

"I had a good time, Grace," he said. "Thanks."

"Yeah, thanks," Grace replied easily, hitting him lightly on his well-muscled arm. "See you in the morning, superhero."

"I wish you wouldn't call me that," Carr said earnestly.

"Why, not faster than a speeding bullet? Or unable to leap tall buildings in a single bound?"

He shook his head. "Neither," he answered.

"Are you sure you don't have X-ray vision, at least? All night I've had the strangest feeling that you've been looking at my underwear."

"Oh, Grace." Carr shook his head.

"I know—you have to get up early," she said, watching him disappear into the darkened house. A light went on across the den, spilling from his room. And then the door closed, and the light became a line below it. She turned and walked away into the night.

Grace walked all the way down to the amusement park and back, and she still didn't feel any better.

"What's wrong with me anyway?" she asked herself, falling onto a bench along the beach. She watched the waves roll in to shore. In the distance she could see boats out on the water.

"I'm in good health, emotionally and physically," she continued, as though she were listing her assets to get a loan. "Nothing to complain about. I never had a drug problem, I no longer have a drinking problem, and luckily I don't have a sexually transmitted disease."

"I could . . . give you one of those . . . if you want." A figure lurched out from under the boardwalk behind her, falling over the back of the bench and burping loudly. Grace could smell the alcohol on him. It was almost like a fog. She stood quickly.

"No thanks," she replied, moving away.

"If you . . . change your mind . . ." He burped again and fell down into the sand.

"Yep, I'll know where to find you." Grace almost laughed. *But no matter how weird I may be feeling now, I'm never going to feel bad enough to drink again!* Grace thought, wondering which bar he'd stumbled out of.

She walked along the beach, back toward her house. She felt uneasy, but she had no idea why. Her life was basically the same as it had been three weeks ago.

Except for one thing. David.

Grace wondered where he was, and imagined him lounging in an Asian sauna, with beautiful women serving him trays of food and pouring water on the hot coals. She saw him so clearly, his dark hair curly and wet, his face relaxed. "Hey, can't a guy get a bagel and lox around here?" he'd probably ask, pushing away a bowl of noodles. Grace burst out laughing.

It didn't hurt to think of him with other women, because she knew that her fantasy was probably the complete opposite of what he was really doing, which was sleeping in a barracks somewhere with a lot of other men, flying jets all day long. The truth was more threatening, because flying was something he really loved. Perhaps more than her.

Grace kicked the sand and rubbed her face, willing herself not to cry. *I'll never see him again*, she told herself. *Most likely, I never will.*

But what if she did? What if he showed up tomorrow? Then what would she do about Carr? She did have Mr. Superhero living in her basement, no hiding that.

"I wouldn't break Carr's heart," she muttered. "Not with a hundred women chasing him every day."

She realized in that instant how easy it would be to stop seeing Carr. But when she tried to imagine introducing David to Wilton, she found she couldn't really picture the outcome. The truth was, they'd probably like each other. David was the only person Grace knew who might be able to keep up a literary conversation with Wilton. If she'd been with David tonight instead of Carr, he'd have wanted to go with Wilton and try out the telescope.

Grace didn't want to believe it, but perhaps that was why she felt so strange around Wilton. In some ways he reminded her a lot of David. His sensibility was the same—smart and soft-spoken, and impervious to criticism, just like David. David never really cared what other people thought of him. He cared only about what he thought of himself. Wilton was like that too.

And though Wilton didn't have David's smoldering sexy good looks, he wasn't unattractive. It just took a while to see, because he didn't flaunt it, but Wilton actually had a very sensitive face. It was thin and serious, and there was an indefinable expression around his eyes. He wasn't the well-muscled type, but he was fit. Sleek, and quiet.

There was something going on under that quiet surface, though, Grace thought. Maybe that was the attraction? Carr's attributes were all on the surface, but not Wilton's. And Grace couldn't help herself, but she wanted to know what Wilton was like. What was he really like when he cared enough about something to show it? What if he cared enough about her?

"But it doesn't matter what you want to know," Grace lectured herself. "And you may as well stop thinking about him, because he isn't interested in you! He's disappointed in your choice of men," Grace admitted, recalling the tension between him and Carr, the subtle, cutting remarks. "Oh, who cares? It's certainly not as though he's stepping forward and offering himself—is he?"

It hung in the air—the unspoken question that Grace couldn't quite answer. And if he was stepping forward, Grace, what would you do?

Grace glanced up and spotted a familiar figure on the boardwalk. She couldn't quite tell from where she was, but she thought it was Chelsea.

It sure looked like Chelsea, or at least something Chelsea would wear; a brightly patterned jacket tied at the waist with a flaming red sash. Chelsea, or the Chelsea lookalike, was scurrying along the boards, obviously in a hurry to get somewhere. Grace wondered what she could be doing out so late.

Grace turned back and scanned the rest of the boardwalk. She saw a figure outlined in the light of an all-night diner. Grace couldn't see who it was, but obviously that's who Chelsea was meeting.

Grace hoped it was Connor. He wasn't

Grace's type at all, but he was cute in his own pixieish way. And he definitely wasn't the steadiest guy in the world, but he had passion. And so did Chelsea. No doubt life would always be rough for two artists, but it seemed to Grace that they were meant for each other.

Any couple who could get through so many obstacles to marriage must really want to be together deep down. Grace figured their hearts were probably ahead of their brains. What was happening now was growing pains. Being in love was easy. It was learning to live together that was the hard part. Connor and Chelsea were right for each other. Hopefully they'd figure that out.

"So who is it who's right for me?" Grace whispered, hugging herself and finally heading home.

Antonio was leaning against the railing of the boardwalk, the note in his fingers. He was staring thoughtfully toward the dark horizon, the light from the diner behind him casting a strange halo around him. He stood stiffly, watching the breakers collapse onto the beach. He was totally entranced by the scene, and by the time Chelsea tapped on his shoulder, out of breath, he looked dazed, as if he'd just woken up from a dream.

"Weren't you expecting me?" she asked.

Antonio looked at the note in his hands. "What, this?"

"Well, yeah," Chelsea said.

"I guess I don't know what to expect any more," he said a little mournfully.

Chelsea didn't kiss him, or touch him; in fact, she stood a very noticeable two or three feet away from him. She and Antonio gazed at each other from across the distance as though they stood on opposite sides of the Grand Canyon.

"I was at your house," Antonio said.

"I know," Chelsea said.

"You were there, weren't you?" Antonio said.

Chelsea nodded and looked away, ashamed.

"You thought I was Connor?" he asked hopefully.

Chelsea shrugged. "I didn't know who it was."

"Then you didn't want to see me," Antonio said woodenly.

Chelsea didn't need to answer. He wriggled his nose. For the first time, she thought he was about to cry. She took his hands in hers and squeezed them.

"Antonio—" she began.

"No, I understand," Antonio said. "Connor's intense. I think I understand what you see in him. He's very smart—he knows things—"

"He thinks he knows more than he does," Chelsea interrupted.

"Maybe," Antonio said, nodding his head. "He seems pretty bullheaded. But I have to say, I respect that in a man." Antonio laughed sadly, shaking his head. "He got in some good zingers, didn't he?"

Chelsea held back her smile for his sake.

"He's more used to words than you are," she said. "He spends all day thinking about them, working with them. Anybody could have said what he said if he wrote for a living."

Antonio was looking at her strangely. It was a weird sort of calm; sad, but understanding. "I'll be gone in the morning," he said.

"Gone!" Chelsea cried in surprise.

"Isn't that what you want? Isn't that why you wanted to meet me, to tell me it was all over?"

"No," Chelsea said, squeezing his hands. "No, no, no."

"But after what you heard—"

"I know what I heard," she said. "But I don't know how I feel. Antonio, it's a big decision to end a marriage. A big, big decision. Especially for me. You know me—I hate to admit I did something wrong. A divorce would be a total defeat, and you know how I hate to be defeated."

"Boy, do I know," Antonio said.

Chelsea thought she saw a glimmer of a smile.

"But I'd do it if I thought it was the right thing to do," she said quickly. "I want to make sure it's the right thing, not just the easy thing."

She lifted his chin with her finger. "You wouldn't want me to be with you unless you knew I was really sure, right?"

Antonio nodded understandingly, and that impressed her. She wanted to kiss him then and there, but she held herself back. There was a time and a place . . .

"So, what do you want me to do?" Antonio asked. "Because I'll do anything for you, Chels."

"I want you to give me some time," she said. "Just some space. To think. To talk things out with Connor."

"I don't trust him," Antonio said, pulling his hands away. "If he's so good with words, what's keeping him from just talking you into going back to him?"

"Antonio," she said angrily. "I don't care if you don't trust him. But I do care if you trust me. I am strong enough to make my own decisions. You'd better understand that about me. You'd better trust me to do what's right for all of us. Otherwise, maybe you should think harder about whether you want me. I'm not a pushover. I'm not that fifteen-year-old you had a crush on. I am a grown woman now, Antonio."

Antonio smiled. "You sure are."

"Okay," Chelsea said, relaxing.

"Okay," Antonio said.

Chelsea leaned forward and gave Antonio a peck on the cheek. She lingered there a minute, just long enough to feel his warm skin against hers, and to smell his distinctive, masculine scent, but not long enough to get any more funny ideas. . . .

They pulled apart and were quiet for a few moments.

Finally, Antonio spoke. "If you need time and space to think, you've got it, Chels," he said gently. "I'm leaving tomorrow to make a quick visit home; then I've got to get back to the base." He paused, then said, "But we'll keep in touch, okay?"

"Sure, Antonio," Chelsea said. "I'd like that."

"Well, I guess this is so long for now."

"Yeah. Take care of yourself, Antonio."

They paused, not wanting to let go. Then Antonio bent down and kissed Chelsea's forehead.

"Bye," he said.

"Bye."

And they both turned and walked in opposite directions down the boardwalk, he toward the motel, she toward home.

FOURTEEN

At first Grace thought it was raining. *That's funny*, she thought hazily. *They didn't say anything on the news about rain today.* She should probably keep at least one stand open, even if there was no sun today. There were those odd people who *liked* the beach in the rain. Or when it was cloudy. Like Wilton. She could just imagine Wilton waking up and looking out the window to see a storm rising in the distance, then happily bouncing into his kitchen to pack himself a picnic basket for the beach. No danger from the ozone layer, today! he'd say.

That's some rain coming down, Grace thought as she came more fully awake. It almost sounded like hail. The biggest raindrops in the world. *Wait a minute*, she thought. *That's not rain. What is that?*

She opened her eyes.

There definitely was a loud pattering noise right near her head. When she figured out what the sound was, she sat bolt upright up in bed.

Someone was throwing rocks at her house!

She leaped out of bed and grabbed a robe. She went to the glass doors, threw back the curtain, and stalked out onto her small balcony.

"Well, it's not raining, that's for sure," Grace mumbled, momentarily blinded by the sunlight. It took a moment for her eyes to adjust and make out a tiny clutch of bodies that stood below her on the beach.

"Who the hell is that?" she yelled down before she turned to look at her house. "You better not have done any damage," she muttered angrily.

"Glad to see you too, Racey!" a familiar voice floated up. "You always were bright and cheerful in the morning."

"Yeah," another voice laughed, "remind us to crash on deserted islands more often if this is the welcome home we'll get."

And then the last familiar voice. Or rather, growl, whine, and bark.

"Mooch!" Grace shouted, finally recognizing one of the shapes below her. "Justin, Kate!" she called. "Thanks for bringing him back. I was really beginning to miss that smelly sack of bones. No dog hair in my laundry lately. Hang on, I'll be down in a sec."

Grace waved, and turned to go back in, wondering briefly who the woman standing with them was. Probably just another new friend to bring into the fold.

She'd better go wake up Chelsea. Chelsea would be glad to have Kate back now. If anyone needed a few good friends around, it was Chelsea.

There was lots of laughter and hugging as they all converged in the living room. Kate and Chelsea shrieked when they saw each other, and started talking a mile a minute, neither of them listening to the other.

"It's going to take you guys a week at least to sort through everything you just said," Justin interrupted.

Chelsea turned and stuck her tongue out. *Little do you know, you poor weak male*, she thought. "Two weeks," she said, giving Kate another hug.

"I'm glad you're back," she whispered, squeezing her tightly.

"Me too," Kate replied, her eyes speaking volumes.

"It's getting to be a regular thing with you, Justin," Grace remarked, "reappearing just when we're all getting along fine without you."

"Oh, thanks, Racey," Justin grinned. "That really hurt. Did I tell you I missed you? No? Well, good. I didn't."

"I missed you," Kate cried. "I didn't turn out to be the best sailor in the world. I'd just as soon stay on hard, dry land from now on."

"What happened?" Grace asked.

"Seasick," Justin and Allegra said together.

Kate wrinkled her nose and made a face at Allegra.

"You mean you won't be Queen of the Seven Seas?" Chelsea asked, referring to an old childhood game of Kate's; she'd made herself queen of everything at one time or another.

"I guess not," Kate agreed. "I'm going to have to leave that to Justin. He can be king without me."

"I'll be the queen," Allegra offered, laughing.

Kate rolled her eyes.

"Hey guys," Justin said. "I forgot to introduce you. This is Allegra Wolfe. She's a . . . we met her down in the Bahamas."

"She sailed *home* with us," Kate explained. "At least until she crashed us—I mean, until we crashed, that is."

Chelsea and Grace raised their eyebrows in surprise.

"She's a friend," Justin went on quickly. "Allegra, this is Grace—it's her house."

"Nice to meet you." Grace smiled uncertainly.

"You too, of course," Allegra replied, her own smile broad and friendly.

"And this is Chelsea—Chelsea lives across the street."

"Well, actually—" Chelsea began.

"Justin? Is that you, man?" Bo came sprinting into the living room. "Excellent. I'm glad you're back." He gave Justin a quick hug and then a high five. "I've been missing those man-to-man talks we used to have."

"Now, what do you imagine they used to talk about?" Grace asked mockingly.

"I don't think I really want to know," Kate laughed. "Men have some secrets I hope they keep forever."

"Let me help you take this upstairs," Chelsea said, taking the bags from Kate's hand and pulling her away. "I have to put something in my room anyway."

"Your room?" Kate was surprised. "Are you staying here?"

Chelsea nodded sadly, and saw the light dawn in Kate's eyes.

"Oh, no," Kate whispered. "Not again?"

"Again," Chelsea said softly. "But it's not the same as last time." She paused at the bottom of the stairs. "It's worse."

"Well . . ." Bo said, blushing as Allegra leaned closer to him. "We don't have any open rooms here," he said apologetically.

Allegra had pulled him away for a minute, and they were standing on the deck, just outside of the living room. Inside, Grace and Justin were inspecting Mooch and laughing about something. The dog sat easily between them, basking in the attention.

"This is such a big house you live in," Allegra said teasingly. "Don't tell me you fill the whole thing yourself?"

"No," Bo admitted. "Grace is upstairs, and Chelsea, too. Now Kate's back, so her room is full. And Carr lives downstairs. And Roan, too."

"Roan?" Allegra asked, pushing her hair back off her shoulders. "Who's that?"

"She's my, uh, girlfriend," Bo stammered.

"Oh, really?" Allegra said, her voice dripping with disappointment. "That's too bad. I was hoping you might still be single."

"Me?" Bo croaked, his face flaming.

"Sure," Allegra drawled. "I think young boys are sweet. So, you didn't tell me, where do you sleep?"

"In the, uh, I sleep in the garage. That's my room, I mean."

"The garage?" Allegra teased. "One car or two car? Not big enough for one more person, huh?" She reached out and took Bo's hand in hers. "Too bad." She turned and walked back into the living room, chuckling to herself.

"I'd be happy to invite you to stay here," Grace offered, "but I just ran out of rooms."

"There are usually rooms to let in the big beach houses near the south end of the boardwalk," Justin said. "Don't check in the newspapers, though. Just go around to the restaurants and stuff and look at the notice boards."

"I see. I just wish I could be nearby," Allegra said sadly, glancing at Bo. "I don't know you that well, but you're the only people I know at all here."

"If she needs a place," Bo blurted out, "she could . . . probably . . . stay across the street, don't you think?"

"I *don't* actually think—" Grace began.

"What's across the street?" Allegra quickly asked Bo, flashing him another intimate smile. "A friend of yours?"

"Connor," Bo said. "And, uh . . . Chelsea was living there, but she's not right now because . . . because . . ."

"Because she's here right now," Grace finished for him, turning to Allegra. "I'm sure you need a place, but I still don't think—"

"That Chelsea would mind very much, do

you?" Justin jumped in, seizing the opportunity to move Allegra away from him and Kate. "If it's just temporary, that is."

"I really think that we should ask Chelsea," Grace pointed out.

"Ask me what?" Chelsea said, coming back down the stairs, with Kate right behind her.

"Well, I was just hoping to get a lead on where to stay," Allegra said sweetly. "And Bo here happened to mention that you all have a friend across the street—"

"He's not just a friend," Chelsea muttered.

"Well, Justin said that it would probably be fine with this friend of yours—Connor?—if I just crashed there for a little while. Until I can find my own place, of course."

"Justin said that?" Kate repeated slowly, sending him a withering glance. Justin shrugged a little and tried to look away.

"He said he didn't think you'd mind," Allegra continued. "I understand there's a bit of a problem—"

"There's no problem," Chelsea snapped, taking her turn to glare at Justin.

"Okay," Allegra nodded, looking down at her feet. "I'm sorry. You're right—that's a terrible idea. I'm really really sorry. Um . . . I'm sure I'll find something. Maybe you can give me the name of a nice motel?" Allegra blinked hard and looked up, her eyes glassy with unshed tears. "Just until I can hopefully find a job, and a better place of my own."

Chelsea looked at her and sighed. "Listen," she began, "it's just that right now—"

"No," Allegra said. "Really. You don't owe me any explanation. I'm sorry for even asking." She turned to Bo. "I'm sorry you said anything at all. I know you're only trying to help."

Great, Kate thought. *That just makes the rest of us look like heartless monsters.*

"No," Chelsea said slowly. She sighed. "Please. It's not really my place right now to say anything anyway. Maybe you'd better just go over and ask Connor yourself. Justin can take you over."

"Me?" Justin squeaked.

"You were the one who endorsed the idea," Grace reminded him, furrowing her brow and shaking her head.

"Oh, yeah," Justin muttered. "Right. Fine." He turned to Allegra and smiled weakly. "Uh, do you have your bag?"

"Right here," Allegra nodded, prodding the small duffel resting on the floor between her feet.

"Well, let's go then," Justin said, walking to the door. "It may not be that comfortable. You'll just have a couch, not even your own room."

"That's all right," Allegra replied. "I'm good in small places. Remember?" The door closed behind them.

"*I* remember," Kate grumbled after they left. She moved to the sofa, still favoring her ankle, though it was almost completely recovered.

"I have to admit," Grace sighed, "that was the stupidest idea Justin ever had." Then she turned to Bo. He was still leaning in the doorway sheepishly, looking for all the world like he wished the ground could open up and swallow him.

"But it was your stupid idea first." Grace shook her finger at him. "Remind me never to trust my state secrets to you, little brother. Obviously it doesn't take much to get you talking."

Bo smiled weakly. "Sorry," he said to Chelsea. "It just came out."

Chelsea waved him away. "That's all right. It's not your fault. You've already done your share of dirty work for me."

"Does that mean I can be excused now?" he asked, making an exaggeratedly pleading face. "I feel very outnumbered at the moment." He began backing toward his room. "Thanks," he said quickly. "Glad you're back, Kate. Great seeing you. Gracie. Chelsea. Gotta go now—bye." He turned and fled.

"He'd better run," Chelsea muttered.

"Listen, I know it's ridiculous, given the circumstances, and uncomfortable for her to stay across the street." Kate nodded. "But it'll probably only be a few days."

Kate could understand Chelsea's anger. But secretly, though she could never admit it, she was glad that Allegra wouldn't be staying in the house with her and Justin. As bad a suggestion as it was, she understood why Justin had agreed. And selfishly, a part of her loved him for it. He didn't really want Allegra around any more than necessary. If only there was somewhere else to send her, preferably some place far away from O.C.

"Oh, she's not the problem," Chelsea said sadly, looking from Kate to Grace and back into her own lap. "I wish it was that simple. But anyway, Connor's already found someone else to be interested in."

"What do you mean by that?" Kate asked quickly. "You never did finish explaining upstairs."

"Apparently he . . . he's been with someone else," Grace explained when Chelsea remained silent.

"Connor?" Kate asked surprised. "Connor with someone else? I thought this was about you and Antonio. I have to admit I always thought something would happen between you two. But that was back when I used to pretend that B.D. and I would get married too. So what does Connor have to do with all this?"

"It is also about Antonio and me," Chelsea said carefully.

"But you didn't sleep together," Grace reminded her. "It's just not as bad as you think."

"Well, I might as well have slept with him," Chelsea muttered, picking nervously at the edges of a small pillow in her lap.

"Why would you say that?" Kate wondered.

"Because Connor thinks I did anyway," Chelsea explained. "That's when I found out he'd slept with Jannah."

"What!" Kate cried.

"You didn't tell me that," Grace said.

"How could you let him believe that when it isn't true?" Kate said, reaching out to rest her hand on Chelsea's shoulder. "Why would you let him believe something like that? That's not you. And that's not the truth."

"But I wanted to be with Antonio," Chelsea moaned. "I mean, I thought about it."

"But Chels, honey, thinking and doing are not the same thing," Grace said, a tight, sad smile on her face. "Believe me, there's a world of difference between the two."

"Chelsea," Kate said suddenly, gripping her arm tighter. "Connor thinks you slept with

Antonio, but you didn't. Hasn't it occurred to you that you think he slept with Jannah, and maybe he hasn't? Maybe he's doing the same thing you're doing."

"Or," Grace added, "he might have felt so humiliated that he lied about it. What husband wants to find out his wife has been unfaithful? So he's pretending he had an affair too."

"That's right," Kate pressed.

Chelsea sighed, and dropped her head back against the couch. "I wish it could be that simple," she said. "But it's not the same. She's giving him more than that. You have to hear the way he talks about her, the way he defends her. It's his work, too. It's like she's the partner he's been waiting for. The one he always wanted to have. Plus she's older. And she's white!"

"But Chelsea, you should have told him the truth about Antonio. You shouldn't have let him believe something that wasn't true of you," Kate said. "This Jannah person may be willing to sleep with a married man, but you, *a married woman*, did *not* sleep with someone else."

"You *are* still his wife," Grace added.

"I don't know," Chelsea mumbled, looking away. "I don't know anymore."

FIFTEEN

Connor heard the knocking on his front door and shook his head. "Not home," he muttered. *Busy, working. Writing the Great Irish-American Novel. Go away. Leave. Get lost.*

The knocking continued.

"Go away," he growled under his breath, and leaned forward over his computer and continued typing.

But the knocking continued. "I know you're in there, Riordan," he heard Justin say.

"Go away, nobody's home!" Connor cried.

"The windows are steamy with brain-fog, Connor," Justin yelled. "And I can hear you tapping from across the street."

"This better be important," he said, and pushed himself out of his chair and wobbled toward the front door. His legs were rubbery, and he realized he'd gotten up from his desk only once since sitting down to work in the wee hours of the morning.

"What!" he cried, and swung open the door.

Of all things, he didn't expect this: a sexy redhead in shorts and a bikini top that left positively little for the imagination.

Allegra smiled sweetly, and Justin stepped out from the side and stood behind her.

"I thought so," Justin said. "Nice to see you again too."

"Right," Connor nodded, rubbing his eyes. "You've been gone? Oh, yes, sailing or something. You're back now? So soon? Well, glad to have you back, mate. And I mean that."

"I can see that," Justin replied. "But I'll forgive your lackluster welcome. You look like you were working." Justin tried not to laugh. "Did you say you were working?"

Connor grimaced. "I was working well," he amended. "Do you know how rare it is to work as well as I was working? Do you have any concept, Justin, just how hard it is to get into a writing groove and stay there for more than five minutes without being interrupted?"

"Connor, meet Allegra," Justin said, ushering her past Connor to the couch in the living room. "We brought her back from the Bahamas."

But as Justin stepped by, Connor grabbed a handful of shirt and pulled him aside.

"What is she, a souvenir? I'm happy for you, Justin, for getting her home in one piece, but what are you trying to do to me?" Connor hissed. "That editor called me today, wanting to know where my book was."

"And where is it?" Justin asked innocently.

Connor tapped his temple. "Unfortunately, it's still up here. It's got to get on there," he said, pointing to the desk in his bedroom, where a ream of blank paper sat beside his computer.

"I have to ask you a favor," Justin said.

"This'd better be good."

Justin smiled mischievously. "It is."

"Does it have anything to do with—what's-her-name?"

"Allegra. And yes, uh-huh, yes it does."

"What? What is it? Just tell me what it is and let me get back to work."

"She needs a place to stay for a while," Justin said quickly.

"A place to stay."

"Yup."

"And you thought that this might be just such a place."

"Yup," Justin said smugly. "You know, because—"

"Because this house is currently bereft of female inhabitants," Connor interrupted.

"I'm sure it's a situation I would sympathize with," Justin said sincerely. "But I have my own situation at the moment. I was feeling a little guilty about this, but since you showed me how happy you are to have me back, I don't feel so badly."

"Can I guess?" Connor smirked. "Does *your* situation have something to do with Kate?"

Justin nodded.

"Kate and Allegra aren't . . . shall we say . . . bosom buddies?"

Justin shook his head.

"For how long?" Connor sighed.

"Temporarily," Justin answered.

"She can pay rent?"

Justin nodded with profound certainty. "Of course."

"Yeah, right," Connor scoffed.

He glanced back at Allegra. She seemed to be searching the room with her eyes. When she noticed Connor's attention, she flashed him a brilliant smile. Connor thought she was acting a little weird, as if she was searching the room for something she'd left there.

"If Kate has a problem with her, you think Chelsea won't?" he said, turning back to Justin.

"Chelsea knows about it. She didn't seem *that* upset. Anyway, it's only for a short time," Justin assured him. "I don't think Allegra'll be a problem. She's a little bit of a flirt, but she's generally harmless."

"Generally," Connor said.

"Most generally," Justin said, with a glimmer of mocking humor.

Connor glanced at her again. "She looks anything but harmless, you know," he whispered. "She looks like a distraction with a capital D. And capitals for the rest of the letters, for that matter."

"There are worse distractions," Justin said.

"You may be right," Connor replied with a shrug. "But Chelsea's really going to hate this."

"She'll love your accent," Justin said, then poked Connor in the ribs and turned to leave. As he stepped outside, he called back, "I'll just leave you two alone and let you get acquainted. So long."

When the door closed, Connor turned to Allegra and smiled. She had taken an unmistakably suggestive pose lengthwise along the couch and smiled up at him.

Connor cleared his throat, but suddenly found himself with nothing to say.

"Comfortable?" he said.

"I think this place is great," Allegra said cheerfully.

She looks pretty dicey, he said to himself. And no matter what Chelsea may have said, he knew she was probably going to hit the roof when she found out that he'd agreed to it. *Not that I need to care what she thinks these days*, he reminded himself. *It's not as if she's not shacking up with some military muscle-head in some sleazy motel. Maybe Allegra being here won't be such a terrible distraction after all. . . .*

"Make yourself at home," he said. "I just need to—you know—" He pointed toward his room.

"Please, go right ahead," Allegra said. "Don't let me keep you from anything."

Then she scooted down and spread herself over the couch, as if she'd slept there all her life, as if it were already hers.

Then again, he thought, closing the bedroom door behind him, he had a sinking feeling that the whole thing was going to be a load of trouble.

Allegra pulled the blanket up over her shoulder and settled herself into the couch. The apartment was tiny. She could see the light coming from Connor's bedroom, and hear the soft sound of him working away on his laptop. Well, it wasn't luxurious, but it was a place to stay. Allegra had worried that she wouldn't be able to get any help from Kate and Justin. Thank god they had sympathetic friends. Although the ex-wife, or almost-ex-wife,

Chelsea, probably wasn't too happy about Allegra being in her apartment.

Allegra shrugged. Who cared about her, anyway?

She turned to face the couch, trying to find complete darkness. She smelled something funny, and she sniffed once or twice until she realized that she smelled dog. And a familiar dog at that. She sniffed the blanket again. Mooch. Great. Obviously she was sleeping on Mooch's old bed.

Then Allegra smiled slowly. That meant that she was sleeping on Justin's old bed, and *that* made her feel much more cozy and at home.

Justin, she thought, *don't you know that you're a fool to stay with Kate when you could have me?* She laughed to herself. Well, who knew? She'd be in O.C. for a while. She might do better with Justin now that there was an entire city for them to move around in, and Kate wouldn't be watching over their shoulders every minute, with her sore ankle and her whining.

Allegra recalled Kate's face when Chernak's men had started towards them. Terrified. Ha! Allegra was certain she would have found a way out of that mess. She knew Trevor liked her too much to hurt her. At least he had liked her body.

Good old Chernak. Well, we slipped you for a while, didn't we? Allegra thought. She wondered if he had anybody staked out in Ocean City anymore. He had someone looking for her, no doubt. He hated to leave anything unfinished, and Allegra had definitely gotten the best of him the last few times they'd crossed paths.

Well, she wasn't worried. Someone was probably after her, and she had enough coke to land her at least a decade in a federal prison. But she'd found a place to stay. She was tired, Allegra realized, feeling the heaviness sneak into her bones, but she wasn't worried. Tomorrow was another day, after all, and she would still come out on top. She always did.

SIXTEEN

Lying on the couch, feigning sleep, Allegra kept her eyes closed against the sun streaming in the window. She was listening to the sounds of Connor waking up and moving around his room.

"Take a shower already," she hissed, impatient to get up. Finally she heard the squeak of the shower taps and the sound of the water hitting the stall. Then a door slid open and closed, and the water noise became muffled.

"Good boy," Allegra said, rolling over to the edge of the couch. "Make sure you take your time and scrub behind your ears."

She dropped her head over the side of the couch, and her hair fell onto the floor around her. She lifted the edge of the couch cover and smiled. She reached under and touched the large coffee can she'd stashed there last night after Connor had retired to his room. She'd found it among numerous other cans of coffee in a kitchen cabinet, and wondered how two people could drink so much of the caffeinated brew.

She scratched the can with her fingers and grinned. Then she pushed at it to get it moving, and rolled it closer. She set it on the floor and peeled back the lid.

The four little bricks of cocaine she'd brought with her were squeezed snugly inside.

"Taster's Choice," she sighed. "It certainly is." She kissed two fingers and touched each brick gently. Then she sealed the lid back on and rolled the can under the couch.

She swung her legs out from under the blanket and stood up, bending over to shake out her long auburn hair. She flipped her head back up just in time to see Connor stepping out from the bathroom with a towel wrapped around his waist. Steam poured out behind him.

Allegra yawned and stretched, laughing inside because she knew that Connor couldn't help himself. He'd have to look at her, since she was wearing a cut-off T-shirt and lacy underwear.

"Good morning," she purred, her eyes twinkling. "Got a towel for me?"

Connor gulped and opened his mouth, but nothing came out. He cleared his throat and tried again.

"Mornin'," he croaked. "Towels in bathroom."

She came toward him, and Connor slid away against the wall toward his room.

"Thanks for the couch," Allegra said sweetly, catching his eyes against his will. "I was so comfortable last night. In fact, it was so beautiful out, I really didn't even need the blanket." Allegra giggled and blushed. Connor clutched at his towel.

"I didn't really need *anything*," she went on, "but, well, I wouldn't want to shock you if you came out in the middle of the night for a glass of water . . . or anything else. . . ."

"Right," he nodded. "Thanks for thinking of me."

"Anytime," Allegra grinned, leaning up against the bathroom door. "I haven't had time to go shopping, so . . . is it all right if I use your soap and shampoo?"

"Whatever's there," he said. "Be my guest."

"I'd like that," Allegra replied evenly. "You don't have a back brush by any chance, do you?"

"Nope, sorry. Nothing of that sort here. We're just your regular soap, water, and washcloth types."

"Oh," she said sadly. "I guess I couldn't ask you to . . ."

"Oh, no!" Connor croaked, shaking his head. "I don't think so. I'm in a bit of a hurry, thanks.

I'm sure you can go shopping and find something today."

"I guess I can," she answered. "But then I won't be able to ask you anymore."

"That's right," Connor replied. "And it's a shame. Oh, well."

Connor reached behind him and found the doorknob to his room. Somehow he managed to get it open without turning his back to her.

"I'll see you later, then," he coughed out, retreating back into his room quickly and slamming the door. Then he turned and fell back against it.

"Who's *insane* idea was this?" Connor moaned. "Justin's? I thought he was my friend."

This isn't just innocent flirting, Connor thought. *Allegra Wolfe! The name says it all. Basically harmless? Not a chance. She's beautiful, no doubt, but she's dangerous. Very, very dangerous.*

"Just don't cut yourself, boy," he warned. "The smell of blood will drive her crazy."

Connor shuffled to his bureau and pulled out some jeans. He slipped into his clothes without taking his eyes from the door. Then he went to his bed and sat down to wait.

Hopefully she'd leave soon. Connor didn't feel like pushing his luck. He didn't want to venture back out until she was gone.

* * *

"Hey, gang!" Allegra cried from Grace's front door. "Can I come in?" Kate and Grace glanced up to see her saunter into the living room.

"Hi, Kate," Allegra said sweetly, her hair pulled back into a modest ponytail. "How's that ankle feeling?"

"It's fine, thanks," Kate murmured. "And you?"

"Oh, great." Allegra leaned against the couch. Kate saw that she'd gone back to her "somewhat conservative" look: a one-piece bathing suit, a pair of oversized denim shorts, and Converse sneakers.

"I actually came over to get some advice and ask a favor," Allegra admitted.

"What's the advice—" Grace asked.

"What's the favor—" Kate said at the same time.

Allegra smiled stiffly at Kate and turned toward Grace instead.

"I want to go look for a job today," Allegra explained. "And I just wanted to know if there were any places hiring that you could tell me about."

"And?" Kate pressed.

"And maybe borrow something nice to wear on an interview."

"Well," Grace mused, "the only places I've worked are restaurants. Do you do any waitressing?"

"No," Kate answered for her. "She's a little too clumsy for that. Right, Allegra?"

Allegra turned red, but this time there was no smile. "That's just about right, Kate."

"But I know something you might try," Kate offered, "because you certainly seem to be able to swim well. You always did manage to find your way into the water with Justin," she muttered.

Grace raised her eyebrows in surprise.

"And for this job, you wouldn't even have to bother looking for clothes, Allegra," Kate went on. "Why don't you just try out for the beach patrol? Then you'll get to stay in your swimsuit all day. I'm sure you'd like that."

"Thanks, Kate, that's a great idea," Allegra replied calmly, her eyes flashing. "I know you were a lifeguard, but since your ankle is hurt, you probably can't give me any pointers. Maybe I should ask Justin."

"Don't bother," Grace said, wisely interrupting before Kate could answer. "Justin thinks that anyone who needs help doesn't deserve the job. And you don't want to get his vote against you. He's the resident god of the guards, or he was, before the last time he set sail," Grace said. "I swear, to hear Carr talk about him, Justin's ghost still stalks the beach."

"What about my ghost?" Justin asked, coming

down from Kate's room. "Hey there." He nodded quickly to Allegra when he saw her.

"You have to meet our newest housemate," Grace explained. "He was very interested in you, and kept asking when you were coming back to Ocean City."

Kate, Justin, and Allegra looked up quickly.

"What do you mean?" Justin asked.

"I don't know." Grace sighed. "But this guy, Carr, talks about you practically every time we're together. I have to say it's been pretty annoying. Of course," she added, "now that I know you were shipwrecked, don't think I wouldn't have wondered about you myself. He's on the beach patrol too," Grace said. "He ran out to the store, but he should be back any minute."

Just then they heard someone come in from the patio downstairs. As Carr came into view, Grace couldn't help but sigh, and she even heard Kate suck in her breath. It was nice to know that Kate was also susceptible, Grace thought. It definitely proved Carr's universal gorgeousness.

"Hi there, Grace." Carr nodded.

"Carr," Grace said, "I want you to meet some friends of mine. This is Allegra and Kate . . ." She paused while Carr smiled at the women. "And *this* is Justin."

"So you're Justin," Carr said, his eyes widening with interest. He tried to be subtle, but there was no way to mask the once-over he gave Justin.

"And you're the guy who's been asking about me," Justin said coolly.

"Actually, it's a surprise we're back," Kate added. "We were sort of stranded for a while."

"Shipwrecked is more like it," Grace clarified.

"Well, I was curious about when you were coming home," Carr admitted to Justin. "I've heard that you were the best lifeguard around here."

Grace noticed how cleverly Carr slipped in *were*.

"Oh," Justin chuckled. "*Was* I? I didn't realize my career was over."

"Hey, I'm sure it's not." Carr smiled innocently. "I'm just telling you what I heard. Are you coming back to the patrol? It'd be great to work with you."

"You mean to see if I'm as good as they said?"

Carr blushed. "No hard feelings here, Justin. It's just curiosity."

"That's okay." Justin shrugged. "I know the way it is."

And now Grace did too. So all that interest of Carr's was just good old-fashioned jealousy. It was almost laughable. Now that she could see the little competitive spirit Carr and Justin had, there was no reason not to enjoy it.

"Oh, I don't think you know the way it is now," Grace teased. "Remember the crowds you used to draw, Justin? Back in the *old days*?" Grace shook her head and clicked her tongue. "Well, they were hardly a disturbance compared to the masses that gather around the chair of St. Blond the Beloved."

"Grace," Carr said. "I asked you not to call me that."

"He doesn't like any of the names they've given him." Grace sighed.

"Who're 'they'?" Kate asked.

"His fans," Grace mouthed loudly.

"Grace . . ." Carr rolled his eyes.

Grace shrugged. "You'll see for yourself, Justin. Don't say I didn't warn you. You may have been dethroned during this last absence."

"Congratulations," Kate said to Carr, laughing. "That's quite an accomplishment. Though I must say you look like you deserve it."

"I think I need to get to work," Carr muttered.

"Nah, we'll stop teasing," Grace promised. "Besides, we're going out car shopping today."

"You mean you can buy one just like him?" Kate joked.

"Automobile," Grace explained.

"So, how's Luis been treating you?" Justin asked, moving over to Carr.

"Oh, we had names for his kind back home," Carr nodded. "He's tough."

"The toughest," Justin agreed.

"It's a great job, though," Carr began as he and Justin moved away to stand in the doorway to the deck.

"Leave it to men," Grace mused. "They always find something to bond over."

"At least it's not football." Kate shrugged. "That gets old."

"And Luis-the-toughest-bastard-on-the-water doesn't?" Grace complained.

"Is that who I have to go see?" Allegra asked.

Kate grinned broadly. "That's right," she said.

Allegra glared at her. "Thanks," she muttered. "Any other jobs I might consider?"

"Well," Grace offered. "One of the girls who works for me also has another part-time job. At O.C. Day Care, if you can stand to be with little kids all day."

Allegra smiled weakly.

"I'm sure the trials there aren't quite so torturous as the Beach Patrol's," Kate offered.

"Torturous in their own way, no doubt," Grace added. "But they're always looking for help. It's a place to start at least."

"Well, maybe I'll give that a shot," Allegra nodded.

"And you probably don't have to borrow clothes for that job either." Kate smiled. "How nice."

Just then there was a knock at the door.

"Come in!" Grace yelled. They all looked to the foyer expectantly. In a moment there was more knocking.

"Come in!" Grace shouted again.

There was another knock, and Kate said, "Uh-oh. If they're waiting to be let in, it must be a bill collector."

"Or Dracula." Grace chuckled. "You have to invite him in too."

Finally Grace stood up and went to the door. "Wilton," she said as she opened it. "This is a surprise. What are you doing here?"

"I was wondering if you wanted me to work one of your beach stands," Wilton explained, standing uneasily in the doorway. "It is my day off, but, uh . . . I think Julie is sick or something."

"Oh, right. Well, thanks for offering," Grace smiled, "but I got Bo to take care of it. You can still come in, if you want."

Grace brought Wilton into the living room and introduced him to everyone. He nodded politely to Justin and Kate, but when Grace turned to Allegra, Wilton's jaw actually dropped.

"Allegra?" he repeated.

"Yes." Allegra smiled innocently, holding out her hand. "Allegra *Wolfe*," she replied, stressing her last name seductively.

"Very, uh . . . nice . . . to meet you," Wilton stuttered.

Grace cleared her throat.

"Anyway," she said, watching as Wilton struggled to tear his attention from Allegra, "as I said, I got Bo to cover the stand. I know he hates to leave Roan alone on the beach—he's so afraid of those muscley men moving in on her. But it was just one stand down, and besides, I told him I'd kill him if he didn't do it."

"I see," Wilton nodded, his eyes darting back to Allegra, as if he couldn't help himself.

What is this? Grace fumed to herself. *He's noticing her! He never notices any woman.*

Grace tried to shake it off, but for some reason she was incredibly bothered. *He never noticed me like that*, she realized. *What does she have that I don't?*

"Well," Wilton went on, glancing briefly around the room, pausing an extra second on Allegra. "In that case, could I take you to lunch? I am free today, and I actually just read a very wonderful article I wanted to talk to you about."

"What?" Grace asked. *You're asking me out*

after ogling another woman in my own house! she thought.

"I thought lunch," Wilton pressed, "and a nice conversation between two people."

This was shocking. Was this the same Wilton that Grace knew? What had come over him? He was asking her out on a date—at least something that sounded like a date—in front of Carr *and* Allegra, and a roomful of strangers.

Pretty spunky and aggressive for someone who never even looks at her, she thought.

"I'm, uh, sorry Wilton," Grace answered awkwardly. "I actually have plans already. With Carr."

Wilton nodded, his face serious and intent. "I see," he said.

Grace smiled apologetically.

"Well then, perhaps some other time?" he asked, taking her hand in his and squeezing it briefly. Grace's eyes popped open.

"Sure," Grace managed. "Perhaps."

Back home at his parents' condo, Wilton paced from one end of his room to the other. The shades were drawn against the daylight, though he could hear the tide sweeping up the beach, crashing into the sand, closer and closer.

Wilton couldn't stop thinking of his brother. The last time he'd seen him was in a small stifling room, where they had to speak through a wall of inch-thick Plexiglas, watched over by a guard. Wilton had brought him books, but he wasn't allowed to have them. His brother had said something vague about getting in trouble again, about having his privileges revoked for a month.

Wilton stopped and cocked his ear to the sound of the ocean outside. All that strength. All that open water. All that freedom.

People always said that he and his brother looked a lot alike. Wilton turned and stared at himself in a mirror hung on the back of his closet door. He imagined he was looking at his brother.

"Will you ever get to see all this open space again, Pete?" he said. "You will if I have anything to do with it. I failed you once, but I won't fail you again. I promised. I promised my life. I can't screw this up. It's worth more than one life now. It's worth at least two, maybe three."

He'd wondered briefly what would happen to his relationship with Grace. He definitely needed to get closer to *her*, so what would he do? He couldn't think about it. There were more important matters to consider. . . .

He pressed his fingers against the glass. "Can you do what has to be done?" he asked himself. "Can you?"

SEVENTEEN

"Okay, okay," Chelsea said to herself. She was bent over the phone, watching it as if waiting for it to tell her what to say.

The rest of the house was, as usual, empty. It seemed that the more time she spent around the house, the less time anyone else spent there. Was this a hint, or was she just not used to being alone?

"Okay," Chelsea said again, practicing her speech. "Uh, hi Connor. It's me, Chelsea. Yep, your long-lost wife. I was just wondering if it would be okay if I came over and got the rest of my stuff—"

Something wasn't right.

Why do I need his permission? she wondered. It's half my home. At least half. I have a key. I could walk across the street and go on in there and do whatever I wanted. I could stay there and tell him to move out. I could kick him out of the bed and make him take the couch. Who does he think he is, making me ask permission to come over to my own apartment! Maybe I should call the Department of Immigration and give them a tip about a mysterious Irishman who'd been in the country illegally for months. That would show him!

Chelsea was breathing heavily. She started to laugh at herself. It was so easy to pick a fight with Connor, she could do it even if he wasn't there.

"Okay, Chels," she said aloud. "Calm. Calm."

Besides, her second reason for wanting to call was to see if he wouldn't like to talk. In some public place, crowded with impressionable children, to keep them from screaming at each other. *Maybe a candle-lit dinner on the wharf. I could make a picnic basket. . . .*

Chelsea remembered her first dates with Connor—picnics on the beach . . . the sun sitting on the horizon like a giant orange . . . the sky a layer cake of yellows and greens and blues . . . night falling behind them, a deep indigo sea, the stars like tiny ships winking far out on the water . . .

"Wake up, Chels," she said to herself. "Don't forget that you're mad at him."

Those nights felt like years ago.

Chelsea snatched up the phone and dialed. She felt a little stupid punching in the number, not only because it used to be hers, but also because the house was right across the street, not fifty feet away.

The phone rang once, twice—

"Connor?" Chelsea asked.

"You've reached Connor Riordan," the answering machine spat out coldly, "Leave a message if you want. *Beep*."

Chelsea was dumbfounded. She looked at the receiver bitterly and put it back on its cradle. It used to be her voice on the answering machine. It used to be a sweet message, homey, welcoming, that mentioned both their names. In these days of high-tech phone machinery, changing the outgoing message on the answering machine seemed to be the first order of business after breaking up.

"Where is he?" she said. She felt jilted, as if she'd already made their date to talk and he'd stood her up. As if he should have just known she wanted to see him.

Or maybe he was screening her call. Maybe he was working and didn't want to be disturbed.

But he would have picked up for me! she thought.

Unless he had company. Unless Jannah—

And for what seemed like the hundredth time that day, she pictured Connor with Jannah on her old bed, sprawled on her sheets, surrounded by paper, both of their novels mingling and mixing and merging to become one long classic.

She saw the book in her mind, pictured the words "by Connor Riordan and Jannah Britt" on the cover. Their photographs and biographies would be displayed side by side on the back flap of the dust jacket. And in Connor's there'd be no mention of her, Chelsea Lennox, first true love, inspiration, confidante, ex-wife. Chelsea punched the couch, mortified that Connor and Jannah might be laughing at her at this very instant.

"Unless, unless . . ." Chelsea said. She plopped down in the cushions.

Unless that awful Allegra had already seduced him away from Jannah, she thought.

She'd decided she didn't trust Allegra the second she'd laid eyes on her. She was sure it was more than one woman's jealousy over another woman's perfect figure and face. There was something about her that seemed off, even dangerous. It was Chelsea's old sixth sense again—her sixth sense that had never been wrong.

Chelsea reached for a throw pillow and launched it at the wall.

"That's it," she declared to the empty living room. "I'm just going to go over there without asking anyone else's permission, and whatever I find, well, I find."

Chelsea stood, faced the door, and walked out into the sunshine.

From the porch of Grace's house, the big house across the street looked empty. The shades in their apartment window were drawn, the windows closed. No unfamiliar cars in sight.

Chelsea crossed the street, went into the big old Victorian house, and climbed the familiar steps. She found herself standing outside the apartment door, the number hanging askew just as it had been when they first moved in.

Chelsea stood still and listened. She didn't hear anything—no typing, no voices, no laughter—and raised her hand to knock. But she stopped herself.

Knock on my own door? she said to herself.

She took out her key, unlocked the door, and pushed her way into the apartment, into the familiar room, the familiar smell of Connor.

She looked around. Nothing seemed to be new, except a pile of strange clothes in the corner of the living room. On closer inspection, Chelsea saw that they were female clothes—underwear, bras, bikinis, those little halter tops Allegra liked to wear. Chelsea huffed silently to herself. It was one thing to move into some strange man's house, she thought, but it was another to leave your private stuff around. It was rude, and it just wasn't right. She didn't trust Allegra before, and she definitely didn't trust her any more now.

Slowly Chelsea moved through the apartment, touching all her old things: the tiny table where she and Connor ate together, the couch where they'd spent dozens of quiet, passionate evenings. She could still hear the priest's invocations of the power of God: for better or for worse, for richer or poorer, in sickness and in health. Till death do us part.

"Till death do us part," she whispered aloud, feeling the words on her tongue just as she said them last year.

She could feel her throat begin to tighten—like it always did just before she was about to cry.

Chelsea turned and walked across the tiny living room and into the bedroom. She stopped in surprise. It was shockingly clean, the bed made, the clothes put away. It was as if Connor had reformed. As if he was trying to impress her without her even knowing it!

"Yeah, right," Chelsea said. "Wishful thinking."

She turned to the bureau, where she kept most of her clothes, and stopped dead in her tracks. She was really shocked. He hadn't moved the photographs, the dozens of little picture frames she'd brought with them for the summer; the frames that housed the little square photos, the snapshots of their year of life together. Last summer in O.C. Their year in New York City. Laughing faces, smiling faces, eyes full of love—their faces, their eyes. She touched each one, as if by feeling them on her fingertips she could bring all the old moments back to life, as if she could turn back time. She tasted the salty wetness on her lips and realized that she was crying. But she did not stop herself. No one else was home. Why should she? She was free. It was her apartment.

"It's my apartment," she sobbed bitterly. "Our apartment. Ours."

Many long minutes later, Chelsea was filling a paper grocery bag with her things. She picked out three or four of the pictures from the bureau and wrapped them carefully in a T-shirt, then tucked the package in among the rest of her clothes.

She walked out into the living room and looked down into the pile of Allegra's things. She just didn't like it. She didn't think it was right for a strange girl to expose herself like that.

Chelsea dropped her bag onto the floor, then scooped up Allegra's clothes and stood, wondering what to do with them. She eyed the hall closet, and just as she took a step in that direction, the front door swung open, filling the living room with daylight.

"Connor," Chelsea said, smiling.

But a much smaller person walked through the door. Small, slinky, eyes glowering fiercely.

"What are you doing?" Allegra cried. She ran over and pulled some of the clothes out of Chelsea's arms, and the whole pile fell out onto the floor.

Allegra swept it all together and dropped the pile back into the corner, then turned and leveled a malevolent gaze at Chelsea.

"What are you doing with my things?" she growled.

"What are they doing spread out in the living room for everyone to see?" Chelsea countered.

"It's none of your business," Allegra spat. "This isn't your house anymore. It's not like you live here."

Chelsea was blind with rage. "Look, Allegra, I didn't mean to anger you. It's not like I was searching your stuff or anything."

"Well, that's not what it looked like."

"I don't care what it looked like," Chelsea said. "I was just moving them into the closet—where you could have more privacy. It's not very polite to leave your underwear and bras lying all over the place for everyone to see."

"Everyone doesn't see them," Allegra said with a strange smile. "Just Connor sees them."

Something about the way Allegra said Connor's name made Chelsea want to leap on Allegra and tear her hair out. She said his name with such familiarity, as if Connor wouldn't mind seeing Allegra's underwear because he saw it all the time anyway: on her, and maybe off her also. Chelsea decided that her suspicions about Allegra seducing Connor were right on the mark.

"But that's the point," Chelsea said. "Connor shouldn't see them. You're just a stranger."

Allegra folded her arms across her chest and leered at Chelsea. She began to walk around the apartment, straightening things here, dusting them there. It was as if she'd lived there for months, as if the place was hers and not just a temporary stop.

"By the way, Chelsea," Allegra said slyly. "I like your boyfriend."

"Husband," Chelsea spat out. "There's a difference."

Allegra raised her eyebrows. "Oh, really?" She looked toward the bedroom, as if daring Chelsea to explain why it wasn't her who slept in there with Connor every night.

"Well, look, Chelsea. Right now it doesn't seem as if you and Connor are, shall we say, getting along." Allegra glanced down at Chelsea's bag full of clothes. "It looks to me like you're pretty well settled in Grace's house, which means that maybe you shouldn't consider this home for the time being—"

Chelsea felt her heart pound with rage.

"Which means," Allegra went on, "that maybe it's not okay for you to come in here whenever you want, looking through other people's stuff—"

"I wasn't looking!" Chelsea said, her voice laced with helpless frustration.

"Moving other people's valuable stuff around," Allegra said, as if Chelsea hadn't said a thing.

Chelsea and Allegra faced off silently, and neither said a thing for a few minutes. But Chelsea knew she would lose this war of silence, because she knew that it was she, and not Allegra, who had to leave. As much as she despised the idea, it was not she but Allegra who was sleeping here at night. But she couldn't get the thought out of her head that letting her stay with Connor was like letting a fox into the chicken house.

Why had Allegra lost her cool so badly when she saw Chelsea holding her stuff? It was just some dirty laundry. What could Allegra not want her to see?

Whatever was going on, Chelsea refused to be beat. She smiled victoriously, picked up her stuff, and walked out the door.

"Nice running into you, Allegra," she nonchalantly called back over her shoulder.

Halfway down the stairs, she heard the door slam behind her, then Allegra screech and throw something against a wall with a clattering crash.

"There's something weird going on with that girl," Chelsea said to herself as she crossed the street back to Grace's. "And I'm afraid to find out what it is."

Eighteen

"Think of it this way," Chelsea said, leaning conspiratorially over her freshly made glass of iced tea. "Remember that movie *The Hand That Rocks the Cradle*? Or better yet, *Single White Female*?"

"Yeah?" Kate dropped her sunglasses back onto her nose and studied the sandwich menu on the table in front of her.

"Allegra was born for those roles. Granted, she can't pretend to *be* me," Chelsea pointed out. "Not unless she gets herself a membership to the Tanning Bed and turns herself into a raisin. But I got the distinct feeling that I was *trespassing* or something."

"Well, if she thought you were going through her stuff . . ." Kate mused.

"No." Chelsea shook her head. "It wasn't just her stuff. It was like the whole room, the whole apartment, was just *hers*. I swear if I didn't know better, I'd think she was hiding a dead body in there or something."

"You don't mean—"

"Have you seen Connor lately?" Chelsea interrupted.

"Oh, come on, Chels," Kate shook her head. "I don't love Allegra, but don't you think you're jumping to conclusions?"

"What do you mean, jumping to conclusions? She's probably got a Connor pod growing in his bedroom right now."

Kate laughed. "Well, at least we've moved from big budget thrillers back to the classics."

"*Invasion of the Body Snatchers* is not dated," Chelsea argued. "It was a big budget thriller when they *made* it."

"Are you sure you're not overreacting because, as stupid an idea as it is—thank you, Justin—you're just mad that there's another woman living in your place?"

"Look, Kate," Chelsea sighed. "I won't pretend I'm not bothered by that. I can't pretend I'm not jealous. But it really wasn't coming from me. You had to be there. She was like psychotic or something. Really freaked out. Paranoid, suspicious."

"Well, I don't know why she should be worried about you going through her stuff. She doesn't even have any stuff, though she does have one bag full of very sexy underwea—" Suddenly Kate stopped. She looked up at Chelsea and her eyes grew wide.

"Oh my god," Kate breathed. "She couldn't have. No way. Not even Allegra . . ."

"What?" Chelsea cried. "What is it? You're not telling me something—you've seen her make pod people before?"

Kate shook her head quickly. "No, Chelsea. The sci-fi take is off base. Way off base. But it could be something. Remember we told you about that guy putting the cocaine in our boat? Remember that Justin and Allegra were supposed to get rid of it all?"

"Are you suggesting what I think you might be saying?" Chelsea asked. "I mean, do I know what you mean?"

"I don't know if *I* know what *you* mean," Kate said seriously. "But I'm saying maybe that didn't happen. Maybe they didn't get rid of all of the drugs. Maybe Allegra found a way to keep some."

"Without Justin knowing it? And anyway, where would she hide it?" Chelsea remarked dryly. "There's no room for anything else in that bikini of hers."

"No," Kate thought. "She would have had to keep it somewhere on the island."

I'm just going to go and have one last quick

dip in the little pool, okay? Allegra had said that last morning before they left. *I packed up my stuff. This one's mine. Okay?*

"Wow," Kate said, shaking a little. "I can't believe we didn't see it."

"See what?" Chelsea almost screamed.

"Look, if she kept some of the drugs, she'd have had to bring them onto the Coast Guard boat," Kate said, sounding as though that was an impossibility.

"She seems crazy enough to me," Chelsea remarked. "I don't know how crazy you'd have to be, of course. But today, the look on her face—she could've done *Psycho, Friday the 13th, any* of the Freddy Krueger movies—"

"But this isn't a horror movie," Kate said. "If anything, it's a prison movie. It's not about being a killer. It's about ten years, at least, in jail. She'd have to be crazy to try that. I mean, *right* on the Coast Guard's *boat*?"

"Yeah, it is pretty disrespectful, isn't it," Chelsea agreed, "making all those sailors look so dumb. That is, if she really did that. If it was really there under everyone's nose."

"Or just under someone's bed. It was probably in our little cabin the whole time," Kate said. "That gives me the chills."

"So, you think she has something?" Chelsea pressed.

"She'd have to be pretty desperate to try that," Kate admitted.

"I don't really like the idea of Connor living with a drug-hoarding desperate redhead," Chelsea admitted.

"Chels," Kate said soberly, "if she has cocaine with her, I think the last thing she's going to think about is hitting on your husband. What's in it for her, anyway? It's just a place to stay."

"For now," Chelsea muttered. "Let's call the police and get her out. We don't have to say who we are."

"We can't just call without knowing for sure," Kate argued. "Besides, that would get Connor involved in this mess." She paused, then said, "Now that I think about it, it makes a lot of sense, and fits in with her erratic behavior. But we can't just sit here and guess what's true. We have to know."

Chelsea cringed. "I know what comes next, you know. I *have* watched television in this century. Now you're going to say, 'There's only one way to find out.'"

"There *is* only one way to find out, Chels," Kate said softly.

"I know," Chelsea admitted. "I just don't relish the idea of breaking into my own house. And listen, she was freaked out enough when she found me holding her clothes. I'm afraid what she'll do if she finds us holding her stash."

"Then I guess we'd better make sure that we don't get caught," Kate said, looking closely at her friend.

"If she does catch us at it . . ." Chelsea let the sentence trail off.

"Don't worry," Kate said reassuringly. "She won't."

Kate kept watch while Chelsea put her ear to the door of her and Connor's apartment.

"Hear anything?" Kate whispered, doing her best to whistle and look innocent, as though there was nothing strange about listening at someone's door.

Chelsea slowly and quietly opened the door. "Coast is clear," she said.

They ducked inside and closed the door behind them.

"This is weird," Kate said.

"You're telling me," Chelsea replied breathlessly. "Breaking into my own apartment. But what are we worried about? My name is on the lease, after all. Even if Allegra catches us, what could she really do?"

But when they looked at each other, they both knew exactly what Allegra could do. The question was, What was she capable of? If they were dealing with a real cocaine smuggler, other dealers and buyers wouldn't be far behind. The cops wouldn't be far behind. Dangerous people, people with guns, wouldn't be far behind.

"Let's hurry up and get this over with," Chelsea said worriedly.

"Okay," Kate said. "Division of labor. I'll take the bedroom."

She and Chelsea looked at each other. "Why don't I take the bedroom?" Chelsea countered.

"Good idea," Kate said with a nod, and looked around the living room.

The apartment filled with the hushed noises of drawers being slid open and snapped shut, clothes being rummaged through, chairs being dragged, mattresses being lifted and peered under.

"Anything yet?" Kate called.

"Nothing. Just the usual. Connor's red hairs blowing all over the floor like tumbleweeds. How about you?"

"No drugs. But the first three pages of Connor's novel are pretty interesting."

"Kate!" Chelsea cried. "That's sacred stuff. I haven't even seen it. If Connor ever finds out you saw that, there won't be anything left for Allegra."

"Sorry," Kate whimpered. "I just pulled them out of the garbage. It's obviously not the 'good' stuff."

They met back in the living room.

Chelsea tapped her temple. "Where would I hide drugs if I lived here?" she asked rhetorically.

"That's the point," Kate said. "You wouldn't hide drugs. That's our problem. We don't think like criminals because we aren't criminals."

Chelsea winked. "Everyone has a dark side," she said, wriggling her fingers in mock-horror fashion. "You never know what I can be driven to," she said frighteningly.

"Ooh-ooh," Kate cooed. "Help me, please. I'm scared."

They broke into giggling laughter.

Suddenly Chelsea stiffened.

"What!" Kate hissed.

"It's nothing. I just thought I heard something."

"This is giving me the willies," Kate said. "Let's hurry up and get out of here."

They looked around the living room, peering into the cabinets. Kate prodded with her foot into Allegra's pile of sexy underwear.

"Pretty nasty stuff, huh?" Chelsea said.

Kate nodded sadly. "I could never get into these things."

"She's a sexy little thing," Chelsea said.

"Tell me about it," Kate said mournfully.

"There's a message," Chelsea said, standing over the answering machine. "What should I do?"

They looked at each other mischievously for a second. "Well, your name is on the lease, like you said," Kate said.

"And I guess answering machines do bug out every now and then," Chelsea added.

She pressed the play button. Jannah's voice came through loud and clear, and both Chelsea and Kate leaned in to listen.

"Hi, Connor, this is Jannah Britt," the message played. "Just calling to say I can't make it to writing group tonight. Will you do me and favor a pass on my apologies to the others? Thanks. I'll talk to you soon. Happy writing."

Chelsea shrugged. "Sounds pretty harmless," she said.

"Sounds nice enough," Kate agreed.

"Definitely nothing sexy or seductive in that message."

Kate nodded. "Sounds pretty normal."

"Maybe I'm just an insanely jealous wife," Chelsea said.

"I don't know," Kate said. "Seems like the only natural way to be. It's not as though Connor's gone out of his way to show you nothing's going on between them. Just having Allegra around me and Justin on that boat was enough to drive me insane. I wouldn't call myself the jealous type, but when I am jealous, I usually have a good reason to be."

"Speaking of which," Chelsea said. "Let's finish up here."

She and Kate looked around the apartment. "What's left?"

"Bathroom," Chelsea said. "I'll take the kitchen."

Kate opened and closed the medicine cabinet while Chelsea peeked into all the pots and pans.

"Don't forget to look into the toilet tank," Chelsea called. "I saw that once on *Baywatch*, where some dude taped a whole bunch of coke in plastic bags to the inside."

Kate slid aside the heavy porcelain top. "Just some incredibly ugly-looking water," she said with a sneer. "And that rubber floating thing."

They met by the door and shrugged.

"Could I be making this all up?" Kate asked.

Chelsea squinted, as if she was seeing something from the past, something that wasn't there. "Seems like we have an awfully good reason to be suspicious, though."

"It'd be pretty dumb to hide drugs in here, anyway," Kate said. "It's the first place anyone would look."

Just as they were walking out the door, Chelsea stopped dead in her tracks and grabbed Kate's arm and pulled her back in. "Wait a second. There's one terrifically obvious place we didn't look."

As though Kate was reading Chelsea's mind, she stared straight at the couch. It was the old kind, with big pillows and flaps of heavy fabric that draped over the sides, covering the open space underneath.

"No way," Kate said. "Too obvious."

"So obvious we didn't even consider it," Chelsea said.

They looked at each other, then dove to the floor. Kate lifted the flap of cloth, and they found themselves looking straight at a big yellow coffee can. They looked at each other in surprise.

"Uh-oh," Kate said. "I was really hoping we wouldn't find anything."

"Me too."

"Now what do we do?"

"Pull it out," Chelsea said.

"Go ahead," Kate said.

"Why don't you?"

"Because it's your apartment."

Chelsea frowned. "Chicken," she said, then reached under and slid it out. She peered in, smiled a strange little grin, then turned it over. "Empty," she said.

They both visibly breathed a sigh of relief, then burst into laughter.

"Why is it we feel like we're so bad and tough until we're faced with the possibility of the real thing?" Chelsea said, shaking her head.

"We are dealing with the real thing," Kate admonished her. "I know it. I just can't prove it yet, but I will. I promise."

They both peered into the empty can. A few grounds of coffee were stuck to the bottom.

Chelsea shook her head. "He used to say I was the slob. But look at this. Exhibit A. You're my witness."

"He doesn't even recycle," Kate said disdainfully, with a disappointed shake of her head.

Nineteen

"Ouch," Allegra screeched, pulling her ponytail out of the clutches of two small sticky hands.

"That's Patrick." Jenny Olsen smiled at the little boy. Jenny was in charge of the staff at O.C. Day Care, and Allegra wondered how she could still have that happy grin on her face. She was an older woman, with a kind smile and boring straight brown hair, pulled back into a long braid. But this late in the afternoon, wisps of hair that had escaped the braid since morning flew out all around her head.

"He's really a very nice little boy," Jenny explained. "Aren't you, Patrick?"

The little boy stood staring at Allegra with his hands firmly on his hips. He shook his head.

"Well," Jenny shrugged. "At least he does what you tell him to do. I mean, he stops when you ask him. That's just about a second before he actually dislodges a handful of hair from your scalp."

"How wonderful." Allegra smiled tightly. *This looks unbearable*, Allegra thought. But after that guy Luis at the beach had told her what the lifeguard trials were like, she figured she ought to check out the day-care center after all. The fact was, it didn't look like it would be much easier.

While she had been showing Allegra around, Jenny had managed to stop two fights, get kicked once in the shin, dislodge a piece of food from some kid's throat, juggle a crying baby on her hip, take one girl to the bathroom in time, and change the clothes of another little girl who hadn't been able to wait.

"It is a little noisy sometimes," Jenny smiled angelically. "But kids are kids."

Allegra had almost stopped hearing the constant chatter and screeching. If she took this job, she'd run the risk of going deaf.

"And how many hours a week would I start with?" Allegra asked sweetly.

"Twenty, if you can fit it in to your schedule. That's only five hours a day, which would still leave you most of the day to enjoy yourself in town. We can always use the extra help." Jenny smiled.

"And what did you say the pay was?"

"Well, it's not great," Jenny admitted, "since it equals what you probably used to get baby-sitting for just one kid, and here you'll have about twenty. But it's all we can afford. Or rather, it's all the parents can afford. And it's important that the service is here for them."

"The pay?"

"Five dollars an hour." Jenny smiled apologetically. "I hope that's not too little. You seem quite nice. I'm sure you're wonderful with children."

Yeah, wonderful like I'd like to shoot that kid who pulled my hair, Allegra thought. But she nodded at Jenny and grinned.

"I just love kids," she forced herself to say. *A job is a job, and you need one.*

"Wonderful," Jenny said. "I could tell just by looking at you."

Back at Connor's apartment, Allegra dropped her stuff and locked the door behind her. Those kids would kill her, she knew. She'd have to try *very* hard not to lose her cool with them in front of Jenny or any of the other workers. But a job was a job. And money meant she could pay rent, which meant that Connor couldn't throw her out. And she needed a place for herself and her stash.

Speaking of stash, Allegra smiled, heading straight for the couch. She bent down and flipped up the cover that trailed onto the floor, and before she could control herself, a shriek escaped her lips. She started to shake uncontrollably.

"Oh my god," Allegra moaned. "Oh my god."

She was looking under the couch where there should have been a big fat coffee can on its side, waiting for her. But there was nothing. Nothing but dust balls and an old ballpoint pen.

Allegra rose stiffly to her knees and clutched her chest. Her heart was pounding.

Someone had stolen her stash. Her head whipped around quickly, wondering if someone might still be in the apartment. She rose shakily and stood panting in the living room. Kate? Chelsea?

No way. Allegra shook her head. They'd have already called the cops. She'd be in handcuffs by now, one phone call away from a jail cell.

Maybe it's been misplaced. Maybe moved. Allegra started pacing the living room, her head sweeping back and forth as though she had radar. There was nothing. Nothing at all.

She checked the bathroom, slamming through the cabinets under the sink, pawing at the towels in the tiny closet. She shook her head. Nothing.

The kitchen was small, and it took only a minute to check the cupboards. She even checked the refrigerator. And the freezer. Nothing.

Allegra fell back against the refrigerator. She banged her head against the door. Once. Twice. Again. Tears were forming in her eyes now, and they weren't show tears. Or game tears. These were tears of frustration and anger.

"How could this have happened?" she cried out. "I've been so careful."

No one knew about her stash, not Kate or Justin or Chelsea or Connor. Who could know anything at all about the drugs?

Suddenly she froze. Of course, it had to be Chernak. She'd figured he'd have somebody on this end to get the pickup. But since the crash, she'd thought he might have given up.

Obviously the jerk knew her better than she thought.

This was Chernak's man. Or woman. Whoever took her drugs was on his payroll. Allegra knew it in her bones.

She was about to stalk out of the kitchen when her eyes fell on the garbage can. She sucked in a breath. Next to the garbage was a small blue-plastic tub. Stenciled in white on the front was RECYCLE! And lying on top of some aluminum-and-plastic Chinese-food containers, a couple of empty dark-brown beer bottles, and a few washed-out cans of El Paso refried beans was the extra-large "Value-Size" Taster's Choice coffee can.

Allegra walked toward it slowly, hardly daring to hope. Instantly her hopes were crushed as she hefted the light and obviously empty can in her fingers. She pried off the plastic top and looked inside.

Empty.

She wanted to cry again, she wanted to scream. Instead, in instant fury, she spun around and threw the empty can against the wall. It exploded off the wall, chipping the paint and knocking some canned food and a bottle of cooking oil from a shelf.

They took the stash, Allegra thought, but did they touch anything else? She glanced around the apartment, but everything was still in its place: stereo, TV, VCR. It didn't seem like this was your run-of-the-mill robbery. Whoever had broken in had had a mission, Allegra thought, and the mission was definitely accomplished.

"I've got to get out of these clothes," she said to herself. "Then I'll be able to think more clearly." She grabbed her duffle bag from the corner of the room and unzipped it. Lying on top was a sealed envelope.

"What in the world . . ." Allegra tore open the envelope and read the neatly typed note inside: *Don't be afraid. We'll work it out.*

Someone had stolen her drugs, and they didn't want her to be afraid? Who were they kidding?

"'We'll work it out,'" Allegra read aloud. "'We'll work it out,' huh? I guess that means whoever you are, you're *not* running back to Chernak."

Allegra pursed her lips in careful thought. There was a new stage to this game now. Maybe she could still win, if she could figure out who this was who wanted to deal.

She laughed. Yeah, sure. She'd deal. Just as long as it took her to get the stuff back and get the money. For herself. That was about the only deal Allegra was willing to make. But she'd keep playing the game. She was good at playing the game.

But not alone, she thought, wandering back into the tiny living room and looking around. No matter who was across the street at Grace's house, she'd put up with them. Even Kate.

In fact, if this situation blew up, it would be a bonus to have Kate around. Allegra needed other bodies around. Other bodies that could make good hostages. Or good shields.

* * *

Chelsea walked north along the beach, past the cheesy fast-food stalls, past the mid-range apartment complexes, toward the north end of Ocean City. This was the ritzy part of town, where the big-money condos let out directly onto the beach. Inside the tall fences were other worlds, with pools and fountains and perfectly manicured hedges. She knew where she was going. She was going to Jannah Britt's place, whose address was smack in the middle of all that poshness.

Chelsea was nervous. Not because she was entering the snooty end of town, but because she was about to find out once and for all the truth about Connor and his mysterious writing "tutor." For the last few days, she'd regretted the way she and Connor had "confessed" to each other.

She knew, for instance, that Connor thought she had slept with Antonio; and that he thought this because Chelsea had wanted him to. She not only had dropped hints here and there, but oh-so-carefully had left out important pieces of information. She hadn't denied anything, and in not denying anything, she had made everything seem possible.

She had wanted to make him jealous, to want her more, to give her another reason she shouldn't think about Antonio. But it backfired.

So, she wondered, if that's what she'd done, maybe Connor had done the same thing.

Besides, Jannah's voice on the answering machine didn't sound sexy in any way. Chelsea knew what a woman sounded like when she was having an affair: dreamy, seductive, a little flighty, a little kooky. Jannah sounded serious and direct. Like a friend, not a lover.

But she wouldn't believe a thing unless she heard it from the source herself.

Jannah's condo was on the left. Chelsea spotted the long sliding glass door that let out onto the sand and the waves and all that distance to the horizon.

"Tough life," she said to herself. But, she thought, Jannah was older. She'd probably worked hard to get where she was now. Sometimes Chelsea had to remind herself that the whole world wasn't twenty years old and living hand-to-mouth.

Chelsea peered through the glass and knocked three times. In the back of her mind she wondered whether she'd catch Connor there, but when she saw Jannah surface from a dark room, she felt guilty.

There was no denying it: Jannah was beautiful, though in a been-around-the-block sort of way. Long auburn hair, piercing blue eyes.

From the look of her, she didn't seem like the kind of person who played games.

It also appeared that Chelsea had caught her in the middle of work. A pencil was stuck above her ear. She held sheets of typing paper in either hand. And she looked confused, squinting at Chelsea through the glare of her glass door, as though she'd just been yanked out of the world on her writing desk into the world outside.

Jannah slid open the door and smiled. Just from the smile, Chelsea thought she could feel comfortable with her. And she saw why Connor would feel comfortable with her too.

"May I help you?"

Chelsea cleared her throat. She held out her hand. "I'm Chelsea Lennox," she said firmly.

Jannah nodded and shook Chelsea's hand. "Aha, the mystery woman. I was wondering when I'd get a chance to meet you. Come on in."

"Are you sure I'm not disturbing anything?" Chelsea said, peering by Jannah into the cavernous living room. "You're not writing or anything, are you? I've learned the consequences of interrupting a writer at work."

Jannah laughed, then sighed. "Unfortunately, I'm always working. But it's not an interruption. It's a welcome intermission. I was just working on a real tear-jerker scene anyway, and could use a break from all that sobbing. Come on in. I made some fresh lemonade this morning."

Chelsea followed Jannah inside, marveling at the beauty of the condo. Big posters—blown-up versions of book covers—took up most of the wall space.

"Those were my first books," Jannah said, noticing where Chelsea was staring. "My publisher gave me the posters. Of course, I couldn't hang them until my ex-husband moved out."

Chelsea raised her eyebrows. "Ex-husband?"

Jannah laughed. "That's a long saga," she said. "To make a long story short, he was a writer too. We should have known two writers living together never could have worked. One of us was always doing better than the other, which caused all sorts of friction and jealousy. When my novels started taking off, my husband really began to resent it, which is why I could never hang the posters. Jealousy—it's not a healthy ingredient for a marriage, is it?"

Chelsea could only nod.

"I tell Connor all the time that he's lucky he's not involved with a writer. An artist is one thing, a writer another. He has great admiration for your work, did you know that?"

"No, not really," Chelsea said shyly.

"Really?" Jannah shrugged. "Well, he talks about you all the time."

"He does?" Chelsea said, surprised.

Jannah looked at her strangely. "Why should that be such a surprise? I mean, you are his wife, aren't you?"

"Yes, but—but—I thought—" Chelsea hesitated.

Jannah's eyes focused in on Chelsea's face like laser beams. Then she nodded, as though she'd just figured something out.

"Maybe we should sit down," Jannah said. "Let me get that lemonade."

While Jannah disappeared into the kitchen, Chelsea looked around the room. The walls were clean white and the carpet was peach colored, soothing, cozy. The color gave her the feeling of peace and security, like the inside of some meditation hall. The big leather furniture was not ostentatious but snug.

So this was where Connor was spending all his time, she thought. Who can blame him? It beats hanging out in our apartment by a long shot. And Jannah's a sophisticated woman, a switch from our always-on-the-brink twentysomething friends.

"This is a beautiful place," Chelsea said when Jannah returned. "I really like the color. It gives me a warm, secure feeling."

Jannah smiled and put down the tray. "Please help yourself." She turned and looked around the room herself. She squinted upward, as if something important was written high on the walls. "I met this incredible older woman a long time ago," she said. "She'd had enormous tragedy in her life. She'd lost two husbands and a daughter to freak accidents. If I were her, I would have been a wreck. But she was holding on. And her saving grace, she said, was her home, which she always painted exactly this color. She said the color gave her serenity and hope in the face of anything. Since then, I've taken this color with me everywhere I've moved. Writing's a hard way to live your life. This apartment sort of makes it easier, I guess."

Chelsea smiled. She hoped that ten years from now she was as together and beautiful as Jannah seemed to be.

"So, Chelsea, what about you? What brings you to my humble abode today?"

Chelsea swallowed hard. "I feel like a total fool," she stammered.

Jannah became serious and leaned forward. "Don't," she said. "What can I do for you? Does it have something to do with Connor?"

"You could say that. I—um."

Jannah held up her hand. "Wait, Chelsea. Maybe I can help you out. Let me confess something here."

Chelsea stopped breathing. Confess? So she and Connor had been together after all!

"I know you and Connor are going through a bad patch," she said. "Believe me, I know what it's like to be on the outs with someone you love. But you and Connor—I haven't even met you before today—but I have this feeling about you two."

"What has he told you?" Chelsea said coldly.

Jannah waved her hand. "Not much specifically. Just that you weren't communicating too well, and that he knew his writing was getting in the way. Believe me, I know what it's like for work to get in the way of a relationship, and mostly that's what he and I talk about. That and his work. He's an incredibly talented guy, but I guess you already know that."

"And you and him?" Chelsea asked tentatively.

"And me and him what?"

"You and him—you know—" Suddenly Chelsea leaped to her feet. "God, I feel stupid barging in here and interrogating you like this. I'm really sorry. All this is my fault."

"Sit down, Chelsea," Jannah said firmly. "Now, I like Connor a lot. I care about him. And if I care about him, I care about you. So why don't you tell me just straight out what you're trying to say."

Chelsea leveled her gaze at Jannah. "Okay. What I want to know is, are you and Connor sleeping together?"

Jannah didn't move. She didn't blink. She just focused in on Chelsea as if she were observing her.

"What makes you think we are?" she asked evenly.

"Just tell me," Chelsea pleaded. She could feel her eyes welling with tears. "I can't take this much longer. I have to know. I can take anything except all this game playing. Just tell me the truth, Jannah. Are you and Connor sleeping together?"

Jannah slid forward in her chair and took Chelsea's hand in both of hers. "I am very fond of Connor, Chelsea. And I completely understand why any woman, you in particular, would be crazy about him. But he and I are not sleeping together. Our relationship is one hundred percent platonic. And to be completely honest, though he's quite a handsome guy, he's a little young for me."

Chelsea fell back into the welcoming cushion of the big leather couch. She felt a hundred pounds lighter, as if a crushing burden had been lifted from her shoulders. Suddenly the day seemed brighter, the sand outside more colorful, the water more inviting. She began to laugh. She began to laugh uncontrollably.

Then she began to cry. One burden lifted, but another fell like a ton of bricks. Guilt. While Connor had let her think he and Jannah were having a raucous affair, she didn't exactly go out of her way to deny that she and Antonio were doing the same thing.

"What's wrong now?" Jannah asked, alarmed.

"I'm such a jerk!" Chelsea cried. She leaped up. "Jannah, it was great meeting you, you're an amazing person, and I hope you and I can be good friends, but right now I've got to go. I've got to see Connor."

"Is there something I can do?" Jannah said, getting up and leading Chelsea to the door.

Chelsea grabbed Jannah's hands, her face streaked with tears. "If you see Connor before I do, just tell him I love him madly."

Then Chelsea ran out. Halfway down the beach, she turned and saw Jannah watching her go, her white caftan flowing behind her as if she were some desert princess. They waved at each other; then Chelsea turned and sprinted home.

TWENTY

"Forgive me for saying this," Kate said as she stood over Chelsea, who was hiding her head under Kate's pillow. "But you're a complete bonehead," Kate said.

"I'm just a jealous nutcase," Chelsea agreed, sitting up with an enormous grin on her face.

"I wouldn't go that far," Kate said. "I wouldn't say you're a nutcase."

"Ha ha," Chelsea whined. "But I will say one thing. Jannah Britt is one classy lady. If she weren't so on top of things, I'd have more reason now than I did before to be worried."

"It sounds like this Jannah person has too much respect for you to ever let anything happen with Connor," Kate said.

"You know, it's funny," Chelsea said dreamily. "I really think Jannah and I can become good friends. It's like we really clicked, you know? It's like Connor wasn't even the most important thing about my going there. I can't put my finger on it. It's like meeting Jannah was a wake-up call or something."

"It was," Kate nodded. "It's ironic that you thought it was Jannah who was breaking up your marriage, when it might be Jannah who turns out to save it."

Chelsea nodded.

"So now what, Miss Repentant," Kate said.

"Now I show Connor what married life is really all about."

"Is that a promise or a threat?" Kate laughed.

"Both," Chelsea said craftily. "He's going to be at that writing thing tonight. While he's gone, I'll shop for his favorite dinner, slip home, deck the place out with candles, turn on some sultry music, slip into some skimpy little thing, sit my butt down on the couch with my legs crossed, and wait for my man to walk on in that door!"

"Whew!" Kate said with mock exhaustion. "I'm tired already! Sounds like we're going to have to send over the EMT's to revive you two tomorrow morning."

"Better not send anybody over," Chelsea warned. "Unless they want to be shamed by some seriously hot loving!"

Kate choked on her own laughter. "I don't know whether to be happy for Connor or to pity him!"

Chelsea peered at Kate as if she was looking right through her. As if Kate wasn't even there. As if she was seeing the scene before her very eyes: clothes everywhere, sheets ripped off the mattress, the temperature in the bedroom spiked to a hundred degrees.

"Both," she whispered.

Allegra pulled her ear from the bathroom wall and rested her forehead against it. Then she went to the sink and looked at herself in the mirror. She knew she was wound too tightly—too tightly to get thrown out onto the streets right now, that was for sure. Her face was incredibly pale and drawn, so pale that the dark circles under her eyes looked almost black. Sick, she thought. I look sick and bruised. Altogether, not very enticing.

"So, Chelsea thinks she's going to save her marriage?" Allegra hissed at her reflection through gritted teeth. "Not if I have anything to say about it."

How fortuitous that she'd managed to overhear Chelsea's plan. She'd gone to Grace's, hoping to find someone at home to hang out with, since Connor had been gone all day and she didn't want to be alone. When she'd heard voices and squeals coming from Kate's room, she ducked into the bathroom next door. She'd heard Kate saying things like, "I knew it" and "I can't believe this." Chelsea was sniveling about her little hubby. *If I were your husband, I'd cheat on you too!* Allegra swore silently.

She couldn't let Chelsea and Connor make up. Then she'd be out of the apartment in a flash. And Kate would *never* let her back into this house. Kate had been nice enough since they'd gotten back to O.C., but Allegra knew if she tried to move in here, Kate would flip out.

"As long as Kate doesn't feel threatened, she won't badmouth you," Allegra lectured her image. "You've got to keep your place at Connor's—wife or no wife. You've got no friends here, and no defenses."

Until she found out what had happened to her drugs and who had left the mysterious note, Allegra didn't plan on being alone. Being alone meant being vulnerable. She had to do something, and do it fast.

Allegra checked her watch. It was just past five. She had to figure out a plan fast, before Chelsea got to the apartment and kicked her out.

She ran some warm water and splashed her cheeks and forehead with shaky fingers. She grabbed a towel and dried her face vigorously, then stopped to examine herself in the mirror.

Now her skin was flushed as if she'd been exercising. She drew her fingers through her rich red-brown hair, took a deep breath, and stuck out her chest. She batted her eyes and practiced one of her sultry smiles. At least she didn't look like Dracula's latest victim anymore.

And her figure was great. In the dark, with all of it to admire, who would have a chance to notice the desperation in her eyes?

TWENTY-ONE

Grace and Carr fell though the front door, laughing, bags under their arms, their hair windblown from driving in Grace's convertible.

"Carr, is that you?" Chelsea asked, poking her head from the kitchen and catching them in the foyer. She was cradling the phone with her hand over the receiver. "It's . . . Jody's on the phone. Do you . . . want me to tell her anything? Are you out?"

Carr glanced at Grace questioningly. Okay, another day spent together. Another completely fine day, Grace thought. A nice day with Carr Savett—the Incredibly Beautiful Man.

Grace looked at him and saw the confusion on his face. Carr was sweet and he was sexy. There was no denying that. But he wasn't someone Grace would ever fall in love with. She knew that now. And frankly, it didn't seem as though he was ready to fall in love with anyone else, either. Grace shrugged and turned away.

"I . . . uh . . . I guess I'll take it," Carr muttered sheepishly. "Can you tell her to hang on? I'll pick up in my room."

"Sure," Chelsea replied.

Carr turned to Grace and smiled. "Thanks for another great day. It was fun."

"It was," Grace agreed amiably.

"I'll, uh . . . see you later, then," he said as he passed her and headed toward his room. A moment later Chelsea replaced the phone on its hook and smiled at Grace.

"Still the old girlfriend, huh?" she asked.

"Yeah," Grace sighed, leaning back against the front door and dropping her bags at her feet. "But that's no great loss. There's physical attraction, of course. But not much else. Even if some people think looking good together is all that matters."

"Now, what idiot would believe something like that?" Chelsea chuckled. "Besides an idiot like me?"

"Wilton, of all people," Grace answered. "I didn't peg him for being that shallow."

Chelsea's brow crinkled. "Wilton said that, did he?"

"Yeah." Grace sighed.

"Well, then he's probably here to apologize for his momentary lapse of stupidity."

Grace stood abruptly. "What do you mean, he's here?"

Chelsea shrugged and grabbed her purse from the counter. "He's been here all day, practically. Very patient, that Wilton."

"What do you know," Grace muttered. "I wonder what's so important. Where are you going, anyway?"

"Oh, I've got some errands to run," Chelsea said, smiling as she opened the front door. "I'm going home to see my husband tonight."

"Really?" Grace smiled, reaching out to squeeze her arm. "That's great, Chelsea. Though why you want to forgive a generally unrepentant moody Irish prankster is a mystery to me," Grace teased, relieved that Chelsea and Connor seemed to have solved their problems. "But as you say, he is your husband, so have a good time."

"We will," Chelsea promised. "He's in for the surprise of his life."

Chelsea closed the door, and Grace picked up her bags and walked toward the living room. Sure enough, there was Wilton, sitting stiffly in one of the beige leather couches.

"Wilton," Grace said coolly. "You look comfortable. What are you doing here?"

Wilton coughed to clear his throat. "I, uh . . . brought you something." He lifted the book that was perched carefully on his lap. "We were talking about it . . . last week, I think. After you finished *The Age of Innocence*, remember? This is another Edith Wharton book I told you about. It's called *Summer*. You said you wanted to read it."

"You came over to bring me a book?" Grace asked blankly. "How long have you been here, Wilton? Not since I saw you this morning, I hope."

"No." He shook his head. "I left for a while. I had some stuff to do. I just came back a few hours ago, I guess."

"You waited a few hours just to give me a book?"

"I wasn't busy," Wilton explained. "I didn't mind waiting."

"Okay," Grace sighed. "Whatever you say. I have to take this stuff upstairs. You may as well come up. You're the one who organized my bookshelf, so you know my books better than I do. If it's a loaner, I'd hate to file it away where I couldn't find it again."

Wilton followed her up the stairs to her room. Grace dumped her bags on the floor by her bed and turned to find Wilton bending down by her bookcase to slide Edith Wharton into her assigned space.

When he stood up and turned to her, Grace had her hands on her hips. She stared at him calmly.

"All right," Grace said evenly, "that's enough

of this. Why don't you tell me what you really came over for."

"What do you mean?" Wilton asked, holding her gaze steadily. "I came to bring you a book."

Grace shook her head. Suddenly, before she even knew why, her heart was pounding rapidly and she realized she was nervous.

"That's a lie, Wilton, and you know it," she managed to say. "You were waiting in my living room. That book is an obvious pretext. I know it and you know it. So just tell me why you're really here."

"I'm not sure if I can," Wilton said slowly, his gaze never leaving hers. He took a step toward her.

"You've never been at a loss for words," Grace pointed out.

Wilton sighed. "I may be now, though," he said softly. "I don't know if there are words to tell you what I'm feeling. I've read a lot of speeches, a lot of declarations, but I've never felt like saying them myself. Until now."

"I don't know what you mean," Grace whispered, watching as Wilton moved even closer.

He reached out and touched her cheek. He let his fingers trail down her face, down her neck, along her shoulder, and Grace felt a shock pass through her. His hand fell back to his side.

"You're really beautiful, you know that? Of course you do. All you have to do is look in a mirror to see how beautiful you are. So I can tell you that you're beautiful, but it hardly matters. I'm not handsome like that," Wilton said, looking down at her floor, both of them suddenly picturing Carr on the phone to his girlfriend.

"Why do you think that's all I care about—" Grace started to say, but Wilton cut her off.

"I'm not a lifeguard," he said quickly, his voice rising. "That's for sure. I don't have the tan, or the body, or the face. But I care about you, Grace. You're the most intelligent and wonderful woman I've ever known."

"Intelligent and wonderful," she echoed, thinking that those had probably never been the first two adjectives to leap to anyone's mind when thinking about her.

"And sexy. Ridiculously sexy. Unreasonably sexy," Wilton admitted.

"But you never look at me if you can help it," Grace said, shaking her head, not quite believing what she was hearing.

"It's because I can't bear to look at you," Wilton explained. "It hurts. The Great Books can't quite prepare you for that," he muttered. "Remember the night you had your party. I hardly knew you at all, and I was up here messing around with your bookshelf because I just didn't know what to do downstairs with a bunch of strangers? You were the only one I wanted to talk to, but you were so unhappy. That was the night your boyfriend left."

"I remember." Grace nodded, looking into Wilton's eyes and thinking, finally, how beautiful they were. How calm. How deep. How completely open.

"You told me once that I didn't have to read about life to experience it," Wilton reminded her. "You said there was enough heartache in the world without *Madame Bovary*."

"I have to tell you something. . . . I never . . . I never read *Madame Bovary*," Grace admitted, her face turning red.

"So," Wilton smiled, "you saw the movie. Who cares? The point is that you were right, Grace."

Wilton took both of her hands in his. Grace could feel that he was shaking a bit, even though his voice was calm. At least, she thought that it was Wilton who was shaking.

"I know about that heartache now. You break my heart every time I see you, Grace," Wilton mumbled. "And I can't stand seeing you with someone else anymore."

"Wilton—"

He shook his head and put his finger to her lips. "No more hints, Grace," he said. "Just let me."

He took her chin in his hand. He tipped her face down and leaned toward her. She felt his lips against her eyelid.

"I don't want to read about it anymore," he whispered, moving his head to kiss her other eye. "I don't want to dream about this anymore. Let me kiss you?" he asked quietly.

Grace nodded, her eyes closed. Wilton pressed his lips to hers softly. Gently. It was hardly smooth, not even very seductive. It was just a kiss.

But somehow it was explosive. And it was the sweetest kiss Grace had ever been given.

"It's about time you said something to me, you know," Grace sighed.

"It took me a while to piece it together," Wilton replied. "I had to read a lot of books."

"What—!" Grace started to pull away, but Wilton put his hands on her arms and stopped her.

"I'm kidding," he said softly.

"In that case you can kiss me again," Grace offered.

"Unfairly sexy," Wilton said, shaking his head but leaning toward her again.

Her lips under his smiled, and she began to hum a familiar tune.

Twenty-Two

"Nick at Night," Wilton suggested as Grace flew through the channels with the remote control.

"You love that channel, don't you?" She laughed, lying back on his couch, her feet up on the coffee table. When she was done with the thirty-second surf, she turned to Nick at Night just as the *F-Troop* theme song came on.

"I think this is déjà vu," Grace said, looking around. "I can't believe it. I'm here in your condo, *again*, watching *F-Troop*, *again*. How *did* you get me to come home with you? I think your serious, I'm-not-interested-in-women-just-my-Great-Books look is just a front, right? You're really very sly, aren't you?"

"*F-Troop* is unique," Wilton explained, ignoring her teasing. "It's in a class by itself. You first start watching it, and you wonder, what's the big deal? How does this reflect our culture? On the surface it appears pretty stupid actually. But it's quite humorous and ironic."

"How *do* you keep that straight face of yours?" Grace marveled. "Anyway, I've heard people say the same thing about *Melrose Place*."

"Well," Wilton said. "I might watch that, too. On a Stupid TV Night."

"And what exactly is Stupid TV?" Grace wondered.

"You know, you're home late, maybe a little disoriented from reading all day—"

"Or hanging out on the beach like a normal person," Grace added.

"And you're not quite tired enough for sleep. Maybe you're eating dinner or something. And you need impulses, stimuli—you need to keep feeding your brain."

"So you watch Stupid TV," Grace finished.

"Yup," Wilton agreed. "Like testimonials for hair-growth tonic, bad interviews with starlets, home-video shows, those programs where you're riding around in a real police car watching cops arrest people all night, usually for incredibly ridiculous reasons . . ."

"I like watching the cop shows every once and a while," Grace admitted. "I mean, who can resist men in uniforms."

"Have I told you yet that I'm glad you came over?" Wilton asked, smiling at her.

"No, actually, you haven't. And I'm glad I came too. I love that this is what you do on your down time," Grace chuckled.

"Well, my routine may be changing in the near future," Wilton replied, trying casually to snake his arm along the back of the couch to get it around Grace.

"Are you doing what I think you're doing?" Grace asked, feigning shock. "Are you putting a move on me, Wilton Groves? I thought you wore yourself out at my place. You still have some more of that impassioned speech-making left in you?"

"For someone as intelligent as you, Grace," Wilton said, his hand finally coming to rest on her shoulder, "I would have thought you'd know that even words have their limits. There *are* other ways to communicate."

"American Sign Language, for instance," Grace said. "A complete language, with its own grammar, syntax, vocabulary. I just read the most interesting article about it, Wilton. You'd probably love to read it—"

"That's *not* what I meant," Wilton said through gritted teeth. "But if you'll just shut up for a minute, I'll show you what I'm talking about. For an incredibly beautiful girl, you sure talk a lot."

"And for an incredibly studious guy, you sure take a long time to kiss a girl," Grace quipped.

"I never told you what my area of concentration was, did I?" Wilton asked.

Grace shook her head.

"I may not look like it, but I *am* the St. John's College reigning expert on the Romantics."

"Is that a band?" Grace teased. "I think I've heard of them."

"Poetry, my dear," Wilton said, shaking his head in disappointment. "I can see there's a rather large gap in your education." Wilton gently brushed the hair from her face and began to lightly stroke her cheek with trembling fingers. "And it always takes a long time to kiss a girl when it's done right. That's so you think about it at least a hundred times, no matter what you're talking about, until you're ready to burst if you don't do it. They call that *seduction*."

"And here I was worried that I'd be scheming for you forever," Grace said. "And the whole time you were just seducing me? That's very bold."

"I'm not bold," Wilton admitted, his fingers brushing through her hair, hovering at her temple. "I'm just terrified of actually getting what I've dreamed about."

"You don't seem terrified," Grace breathed.

Wilton shrugged. "Well, I told you—I've read up on this whole thing."

He kissed her then, finally; her lips were soft and inviting, her smell was intoxicating. His head swam.

This was definitely better than anything he'd ever read.

Later, after Stupid TV, a pillow fight, lots of giggling on the couch, and some more seduction, Grace finally called time-out.

"I'll have to excuse myself for a minute," she said. "Can you direct me to the ladies' room please? I'd like to freshen up."

"Right through the kitchen," Wilton pointed. "I'll meet you back here in ten minutes."

"And where are you sneaking off to?" Grace asked. "Gotta go read up on the next step? Don't worry if you can't find it in a book." She winked slyly. "I'll be happy to teach you the basics."

Wilton blushed. "Just going to grab something from my room."

Wilton left the living room and walked quietly down the carpeted hallway. He pushed open the door to his room and went directly to his bookcase. He squatted down before it and took a deep breath. *Naked Lunch*, by William Burroughs, far left, second shelf down.

Wilton put two fingers on the spine of the book and carefully drew it from the shelf. There in the back, in the darkness, hidden behind a row of books, were four plastic-wrapped bricks, glowing white in the shadows.

Wilton breathed out. Then he closed his eyes and leaned his head against the bookcase.

Oh, Grace, he thought. *What a shame. What an unfair, crazy shame.*

He looked at the drugs again. Trevor had known that Allegra would never let all of the stash be destroyed. And he had known she wouldn't hide it very well. He certainly had been right about that, Wilton thought.

This wasn't much compared to what it was supposed to be, Wilton knew. Chernak had said that the shipment was going to be enormous—the biggest one to hit the East Coast in a long time. Worth lots and lots of cash. And worth a life, Wilton hoped.

But this was all that was left. Four bricks out of forty. Would that still be enough to protect a whole body? Or would Wilton end up with just a hand. Or an arm. Priority Mail.

Wilton shivered and felt sick to his stomach.

All of the threats, the stupid threats. He thought of everything he was having to go through. Then he thought of Grace, and shook his head.

He'd better get back before she came looking for him. No reason to get her mixed up more than she was. It would be harder then, to do what he had to do.

He replaced the book and stood. He'd gotten to his bedroom door when he stopped and turned back around. His fingers skimmed the bookcase and settled on an old volume with worn leather binding. He pulled the collection of nineteenth-century love poetry from the shelf and headed back to the living room.

TWENTY-THREE

"Let's see," Chelsea murmured to herself. She peered into the grocery bag she carried in the crook of her arm. "Cheese, pasta, fresh tomatoes, basil, candles . . . drink!" she remembered, and headed for the corner store.

She smiled as she passed the meetinghouse where Connor's writing group was held. The windows were alight, and she could faintly hear laughter coming from inside. Her heart felt warm. Inside that building was her love, and he was happy, laughing. His work was going well: She was sure of it. He was going to be famous; he'd realize his dreams—book signings, readings in New York City, his name all over the literary journals. And one day she'd realize her fantasies about her art, and she and Connor would be the happy, artsy couple they'd always wanted to be.

And she felt it all started with tonight. Tonight was the first night of the rest of their happily married lives. . . .

She ducked into the convenience store and walked back to the beverage coolers.

"Now, I want something special," she said to herself as her eyes flowed over the liter bottles of Orange Crush and A&W root beer.

"Hmmm, it would be red wine with Italian food, so what kind of substitute can I get?" she wondered. "Cranberry-flavored Snapple?"

"Nah," a voice said behind her. She turned to find a scrawny guy leaning on a mop.

"You work here?" Chelsea asked.

"Sure," he answered. "Now, what are you eating? Italian food?"

"Yep. I don't really want to do the soda thing. I don't think it's quite . . . the mood I'm after."

"Nah," the mop-guy agreed. "Carbonation generally isn't very soothing. Besides, it makes you burp."

"Good point," Chelsea agreed.

"Not romantic." The mop-guy shook his head.

"And iced tea seems very . . . daytime."

"Too beachy." Mop-guy nodded.

"Milk?"

"Too lunchroom."

"And coffee is for after." Chelsea sighed. "With the biscotti."

"You want my advice?" Mop-guy asked.

"Oh, yes." Chelsea nodded. "I think I do."

"I'd go right for the fake stuff," he said. "Basically, you want a wine bottle without the wine." He pointed to a stack of boxes behind her. "That's what you're looking for."

Chelsea opened the box and pulled out a tall, dark green bottle with a red label.

"Looks like the real stuff, doesn't it?" Mop-guy said proudly.

"What is it?" Chelsea looked closely. "Oh! Non-alcoholic?"

"Sparkling grape juice basically, but in the dark, no one can tell."

"Thanks." Chelsea smiled, clutching the bottle in her fist. "Good choice."

"And cheap, too," Mop-guy said. "That's the best part."

"Have a great night," Chelsea said as she went toward the register.

"You too," he replied.

"I plan on it," Chelsea said, turning for the door.

But just as she did, the door to the meeting-house across the street burst open, and out flew a tall young man who looked vaguely like Connor.

Chelsea stepped out and watched the man turn the corner and disappear. No one else emerged.

"It sort of looked like Connor," she said aloud. "But no way—wild horses couldn't drag him away early from that group." Then she shrugged and walked on toward home. *Her* home, not Grace's. She checked her watch. In ten minutes she'd be back in the apartment. Twenty more and she'd have an almost completely homemade Italian meal. She was the one who'd be cutting up the cheese, right?

Then she could slip into her sexy clothes and wait.

"Boy, is someone in for a surprise tonight!" she giggled gleefully.

Connor was almost blind with salty sweat when he ran through the door of his apartment and into the living room. He stood panting in the dark.

His worst nightmare had come true. Allegra had called him at the writing group and cried into the phone that there was an emergency, a fire. And all Connor could think about while he sprinted through the streets of Ocean City was his novel going up in flames. All that work. All his dreams. As easily destroyed as striking a match.

"Never, never again!" he'd screamed at himself while he ran. "I'll make copies of everything and scatter them all over town. I'll get a safety-deposit box. I'll send a copy to my parents in Ireland. I'll dig a hole and hide one in the dirt. Never, never again!"

But now, standing in the living room, he couldn't see a fire anywhere. A lamp was on in the bedroom. Strange, he thought. The light wasn't yellow. It was red. But not the red of a fire—the red of one of those colored bulbs.

And what was that odor in the air? It wasn't smoke, or charred wood. It was sweet, fragrant woman's perfume.

"Allegra? Where's the fire!" he yelled. "You call me out of a meeting and tell me there's a fire, so where is it?"

Connor heard the bedsprings of his mattress creak. He whipped his head around toward his bedroom doorway.

"Hello?"

The doorway filled with a slinky red-haired woman in a transparent silk robe, a drink in her hand, the ice swirling around the bottom, around and around and around. . . .

"Allegra?" he choked. "Where's the—?"

"Right here, honey," Allegra cooed, dropping her shoulder, letting the sleeve of the robe slip off her arm. Then she pulled the loosely tied belt and let that drop, and then the rest, inch by inch, until the robe lay in a puddle of white silk at her feet.